KRISTA'S DOUBT

GEMMA JACKSON

POOLBEG

This book is a work of fiction. The names, characters, places, businesses, organisations and incidents portrayed in it are either the product of the author's imagination or are used fictitiously. Any resemblance to actual persons, living or dead, events or locales is entirely coincidental.

Published 2022
by Poolbeg Press Ltd.
123 Grange Hill, Baldoyle,
Dublin 13, Ireland
Email: poolbeg@poolbeg.com

© Gemma Jackson 2022

The moral right of the author has been asserted.

© Poolbeg Press Ltd. 2022, copyright for editing, typesetting, layout, design, ebook

A catalogue record for this book is available from the British Library.

ISBN 978178199-460-3

All rights reserved. No part of this publication may be reproduced or transmitted in any form or by any means, electronic or mechanical, including photography, recording, or any information storage or retrieval system, without permission in writing from the publisher. The book is sold subject to the condition that it shall not, by way of trade or otherwise, be lent, resold or otherwise circulated without the publisher's prior consent in any form of binding or cover other than that in which it is published and without a similar condition, including this condition, being imposed on the subsequent purchaser.

www.poolbeg.com

Also by Gemma Jackson

Through Streets Broad and Narrow
Ha'penny Chance
The Ha'penny Place
Ha'penny Schemes
Impossible Dream
Dare to Dream
Her Revolution

THE *KRISTA* SERIES OF NOVELLAS

Krista's Escape
Krista's Journey
Krista's Choice
Krista's Chance
Krista's Dilemma
Krista's Doubt

Published by Poolbeg

Foreword

Dear Reader,

This part of Krista's story opens with her being invited into a concealed Benedictine Monastery. I am fortunate to have a monastery not far from my home. The public can attend services. The chanting – oh, the chanting – it is glorious – and it is indeed in French. The monks have a shop on site where they sell their products – candles, essential oils, soaps and creams. I spend far more than I can really afford every time I visit.

I used the monks to underline Krista's homesickness. As someone who has travelled extensively, I can attest that sometimes just a scent of home will bring tears to your eyes. One of the things I have missed most during this pandemic is my visits to France. I so love their markets and bakeries. My mouth is watering just to think about a real French croissant. Not to mention the fact my French language skills are suffering.

I make mention of the fact that Krista cannot find any books to read. Thankfully in my travels I have always been able to discover little hidden gems of bookshops that stock English books. The price might make me gasp but I have something to read which is as vital as food to me. I can't survive without books. Thank goodness for Kindle. It has saved me a small fortune.

Again, the fact that Krista has no home and no family is pivotal to the storyline. As a member of a large family, I have to imagine what it would be like to have no one to lean on. No matter where I have roamed or how long I have been away from home, I always knew that if I was in any difficulty my mother would roll up her sleeves and box ears to protect her young. So many times and in so many ways my mother had my back when times got tough.

I am excited about Krista's adventures. I believe if I am enjoying the stories my readers will too. I hope you get pleasure from travelling along with Krista. I have so many more adventures in store for her.

Gemma

Chapter 1

February 1939
Benedictine Monastery,
London, England

Krista stood before the smiling eyes of the abbot, feeling like an orphan of the storm. What was she doing here? She'd simply wanted to listen to the music flowing out of this monastery and over the wall into the back lanes of this salubrious area of London. She'd had no intention of trying to enter so had dressed for the inclement weather. She was very conscious of her rain-soaked coat and wellington boots dripping onto the immaculate wooden floors of the abbot's study. She was mortified to be presented before this man in her bedraggled state. Still, he was the one who had sent one of his young monks out into the back alley to frogmarch her into his presence.

"Take the young lady's coat, Gaston, and see it is dried," he instructed the monk who stood erect at Krista's side like a soldier before his commanding officer. "We cannot in good conscience send someone out in the cold with a wet coat."

The sweet sound of her native French flowing from the abbot's lips was music to Krista's ears. She removed her haversack and put it on the floor at her feet. She unbuttoned her coat while the young monk stood waiting, shrugged out of it and allowed it to fall into his outstretched hands. She had no idea why she was invited into this room but, since it was Sunday and she had no place she needed to be, she decided to wait and see what happened. It was something different anyway. She removed her woollen hat, scarf and gloves and gave them to Gaston who was holding the wet coat away from his body. He hurried from the room.

"Take a seat, young lady, and tell me how you came to be leaning against our outside wall in the pouring rain." The abbot gestured to one of two chairs in front of his desk.

"Monseigneur, I had no wish to offend." Krista took the seat indicated, her haversack at her feet. "I wished merely to enjoy the music."

"This is not the first time you have been seen lurking in the alley," he said with some amusement.

"Lurking, monseigneur?" Krista caught the gleam of laughter in the man's eyes.

They stared at each other for a moment, each enjoying this break in their routine.

"Tell me about yourself," the abbot said. "I find myself curious about a young French girl who finds her way to my door. How came you to be here in England?"

"It is a long story, monseigneur." Krista settled back in the hand-carved wooden chair, organising her thoughts. "I am from Metz."

"That is a small town on the French-German border, is it not?" The abbot leaned forward, pushing some of the papers away from the lip of his desk so he could lean his elbows on the wooden surface.

"It is, monseigneur."

Krista gave the monk a quick overview of the events which brought her to England. She left a great deal out – after all, this was the first time she'd met the man. She talked for some time, aware of the abbot keenly observing her while she spoke.

"*Ahh*," he leaned back in his chair, "we have heard such stories coming out of France." He sighed deeply. "We are a small cloister but we are not completely cut off from the world around us. So, war is coming once more to that world." He shook his head sadly. "Will man never learn?"

"I am frightened, monseigneur." She had not told him of her voyage into Germany. Some things were best kept to oneself. "The world is not ready for the mayhem Hitler will unleash upon it shortly."

"You truly believe it will happen soon?"

"Better heads than mine believe that Hitler is just waiting for spring before he begins his attack on his neighbours."

There was silence while they both thought of what might be.

"Ah well," the abbot broke the silence, "we will not solve the problems of the world sitting here – much as we might want to." He pushed his chair back and gestured towards a circular table and two chairs off to one side of the cell. "It is almost time to break my fast. I seldom have such charming company. Will you join me?"

"I would be delighted." Krista picked up her haversack. The flask of coffee inside the bag was practically calling her name.

They walked across the small room together. The abbot gestured to one of the chairs while pulling out the second for himself. He waited until she was seated, with the haversack at her feet, before sitting himself.

"Brother Paul makes the most delicious croissants. I will be delighted to share them with you."

"Croissants!" Krista closed her eyes while her mouth watered. "True French croissants?"

"Very true!" The abbot laughed. "The kitchen here is ruled by Brother Paul, a true French artist at his craft of baking."

"Thank you. I would love a taste of home."

"You didn't tell me how you discovered our monastery." The abbot leaned back in his chair.

"I like to explore the streets of London. I was passing one evening when I heard voices chanting in French. It was wonderful."

One of the evenings she spent translating documents for Rabbi Goldstein she'd been late setting out. She hated to keep people waiting so had taken what she hoped was a short cut to the synagogue. When she'd heard the singing she was stopped in her tracks. She couldn't investigate then but had made a point of walking down the same back street several times with the twins. On one such occasion she'd fallen into conversation with a gardener who worked for several of the large houses and had been able to tell her the times she might hear the music. He'd been listening to it for years. She'd had no idea she'd been seen.

A sharp knock on the door sounded. At the abbot's command to enter, the door was opened and the heavenly aroma of fresh-baked croissants travelled into the room. The scent alone almost had Krista moaning aloud. She couldn't wait to taste.

"Thank you, Brother Jean."

The monk unloaded the contents of his tray onto the table. There was a platter piled high with golden pastries, a china pot of tea and cups, plates and cutlery for two. Obviously the news of her visit had travelled to the kitchen.

"*Bon appétit*," the monk said with a smile, and left.

"Brother Paul's croissants are best eaten hot. Enjoy." The abbot gestured towards the platter of croissants. "Would you care for some tea?" He took the lid from the teapot and sniffed. "Camomile, I believe."

"I have a flask of coffee in my bag – perhaps you would care to share it with me?" Krista didn't want to drink herbal tea and spoil the taste of the first croissants she'd seen in months.

"Oh, my dear, you do tempt me. Alas, coffee is forbidden to us." He had an urchin's grin on his face. "But do have some yourself. Perhaps you would be good enough to waft the fragrant steam towards me. I will suffer in silence then."

Krista eagerly retrieved the flask from her haversack.

The abbot picked up a covered pot from the table. "The jam is strawberry. We make it ourselves. It is my favourite." He used the spoon from the pot to serve himself a large dollop which he put on his plate to one side of the croissant. "The milk and butter are from our goats. The monastery is too small to house cows."

Krista poured coffee from her flask. She was practically in tears at her first taste of the crispy, warm, soft, buttery croissant. It didn't need butter or jam in her opinion. It was perfection.

"Now, you have said that you fled Metz?" the abbot said when they had both enjoyed their first croissant and were reaching for a second. "You must know of Herr Baron von Furstenberg?" He bit into his croissant with relish. "The man has a vast estate just over the border from Metz if my memory serves me well."

"I know of the von Furstenberg vineyard – of course I do." Krista wiped her lips with the heavy cloth napkin provided. "I have walked its borders and fields all of my life." She had fled Metz in the baron's company, discovering on the voyage that she was related to him through her natural father, the current baron's brother. She did not mention this fact to the abbot. That was her own dirty laundry and not to be aired in this company.

She reached for her flask to pour a fresh cup of coffee.

"My dear, the smell of that coffee!" The abbot closed his eyes briefly. "It is an occasion of sin all on its own." He examined his guest carefully. He had initially thought the visitor his monks noticed appearing at different times outside their walls was a young man – perhaps one with a vocation to join the order. When the young woman joined him and removed her outer clothing he'd been shocked by her appearance. He could not approve of the latest fashion for young women to walk around dressed as men but then the Lord moved in mysterious ways, his wonders to perform. She appeared far more German than French and when she'd mentioned Metz he'd begun to worry. He had recently – for a very generous donation to the monastery – assisted Baron von Furstenberg to leave England in the company of a group of monks travelling to America. This young woman's sudden appearance in his out-of-the-way cloister was worrying him greatly. If he had understood all that von Furstenberg shared with him, she was just the type Hitler would use for his spy network.

"I do not wish to lead you into sin, Father." Krista liked this man. There was a purity – a peace – about him that was very appealing.

He waved away any mention of sin. "This family who have taken you in – are they kind to you?"

"The Caulfields are a wonderful family. They have been everything that is kind to me, even paying for me to attend classes in shorthand and typewriting. But I cannot stay with them forever. I must make a life for myself." She stared into the abbot's kind eyes. "It is all very confusing."

He laughed aloud at the look on her face. "You are young, my child. I know, I know, an old man patting you verbally on the head. So annoying. But it is none the less true. The world turns not at your command." He was suddenly very serious. "With the state of the world outside these walls," he sighed deeply, "perhaps it would be best for you to stay where you are until the events we fear unfold." He held up one hand when she opened her mouth to interrupt. "Knowledge is never wasted. Who knows where your studies in shorthand and typewriting may lead?"

"I sometimes feel very alone. That is why I was so overjoyed to hear the singing I knew and loved coming over the walls of your monastery." She ignored his comment about her studies with an inner sigh. She could not imagine spending her days enclosed in an office, pecking away at a typewriting machine. She did not like to complain. It made her seem so ungrateful.

"Perhaps you could find some way to use the knowledge you have to assist others. You speak three languages fluently, you tell me – that would be a great asset to many, I am sure."

"I assist a local Rabbi when I can ..." She gave details of her work with Rabbi Goldstein in removing children from Europe.

The abbot stared at his guest in surprise. Who would have thought this young woman had so much knowledge of their uncertain world? "I know of the Rabbi – his synagogue is not far from here. I have heard of what the newspapers are calling the orphan trains coming to England."

"The letters from parents begging for help in saving their children are heart-breaking." Krista eyed the last croissant on the plate. They had demolished the tall stack in no time it seemed.

"These letters you translate – they are written in French?" The abbot held the plate with the last croissant out to Krista – the poor child had been almost in tears as she bit into what was a taste of home to her.

"No –" Krista accepted the last croissant, feeling greedy but unable to resist, "the letters are primarily in German, some in English and a very few in French."

"Indeed." The abbot was impressed. He and his monks had enough to do translating from French into English and English into French. He watched the young girl close her eyes in bliss, popping the last piece of croissant into her mouth. He wondered at what he was thinking. Well, why not? The young girl had been delivered to his door after all.

"Have you somewhere you need to be this morning?" he asked when she had wiped her hands and mouth, sitting back in her chair with a sigh of satisfaction.

"Today is my free day." Krista shrugged. "I have no set plans. I enjoy exploring London on foot. There is so much to discover."

"Good." He stared at Krista for a moment.

She felt as if he were trying to pick her brain from

her head. He had a very disturbing and intent stare.

Then he smiled. "Your legs are younger than mine. Would you be so good as to take the bell from my desk, open the door and ring the bell loudly to call the kitchen staff?"

"Certainly," Krista said, almost tripping over her haversack as she went to pick up the gleaming brass bell.

She stood in the hallway, bent her elbow and the sound of the bell clanging rang around the redesigned stable block.

"*Thank you, my dear!*" the abbot called. "*That will do. We must give them time to respond.*"

She entered the room and put the bell back on the desk before returning to her chair. They continued to discuss life in general. Krista was relieved that he did not speak about religion with her. She was not Catholic. The man questioned her some more about the happenings in the village of Metz. She could almost see his mind working behind his half-lidded eyes.

There was a sharp knock on the door, which opened to reveal Brother Gaston at the abbot's call to enter.

Chapter 2

"You are a very polite young lady." The abbot smiled gently.

They were seated once more at the desk. The remains of their breakfast had been removed and order returned to the cell by Brother Gaston.

"You have never once asked how it came to be that a French monastery should be hidden away down a back street in one of the premier areas of London."

"I did not wish to appear rude." Krista had been wondering but hadn't liked to ask.

"It is no secret." The abbot shrugged. "It is written on all of our information leaflets. We do have to earn a living after all. We make and sell many items which we send around the country." He waved around the area. "The ground at the back of this house was gifted to the Benedictine Order by an English officer whose life was saved by a Benedictine monk during the Crimean War. That was not quite a hundred years ago, in case you didn't know. The house itself is still in the hands of the family but the grounds, the actual acreage of which is quite small, was offered for whatever use we might find for it. The powers that be decided to set up a small cloister here to educate our young in the English language. It has been very helpful for those being transferred to our monasteries in the English-speaking world. It is so much easier to study a language in the country of origin, don't you think?"

"Yes, indeed," Krista agreed. "I have been made very aware of my great good fortune to live in an area where two languages are spoken daily – French and German."

"How did you learn English?" the abbot said. "I never thought to ask."

"There was an English lady living in our village. She took some of the local children for lessons. She made great use of the language tapes produced by the British Broadcasting Corporation – the BBC." She laughed. "I have been assured by the Caulfield maid and housekeeper that I sound just like someone 'off the wireless' when I speak English."

"Indeed." The abbot picked a pencil from his desk and made a quick note on a notepad sitting on his desktop. "I have heard of these tapes. I did not know they were available to the public. I understood they were used for teaching BBC staff British standard pronunciation." He tapped the note with his pencil. "It would be worth looking into. Anything that can speed up the learning process for some of our young monks."

"I don't think the tapes are readily available. Miss Andrews had a connection at the BBC or so she informed us. I could ask her for details if you should need them."

"That would be most kind." The abbot didn't think he would have any difficulty getting hold of the tapes. Not if he asked in his official capacity.

The door at Krista's back was opened without knocking.

"Etienne –"

She turned to stare at the man in the open doorway. He didn't appear to be much older than Krista, probably somewhere in his late twenties. He was casually dressed in well-worn tweeds. He was tall with blond hair and blue eyes and his manner was relaxed, sure of his welcome. This man had dared to enter the abbot's room without permission – *and call him by name* – how shocking!

"I had thought to be here earlier. I wanted some of your delicious croissants but alas …" The man, who was carrying a brown-paper package, closed the door at his back.

"Sylvester, we may very well live in a stable block but there is no need to behave as if you were born in a barn," the abbot said in English, shaking his head but with a twinkle in his eyes. "One knocks before entering a room. Manners, Sylvester, manners."

Sylvester shrugged and smiled charmingly. "I didn't know you had company." He walked over to join them, not at all put out by the reprimand. A slight dip of his head and a charming smile acknowledged Krista. "And such charming company at that, Etienne, you old dog!"

"Sylvester, allow me to introduce you to Miss Krista Lestrange, a native of my home country." The abbot smiled and gestured between the pair. "Krista, this rude individual is Baron Sturbridge, Sylvester Stowe-Grenville."

"Charmed." Sylvester again dipped his head slightly towards Krista.

Krista felt every hair on her body stand erect. Stowe-Grenville? Was this man a relation of her mother's? "Baron ..."

"Oh, none of that, please," Sylvester demurred. "Please call me Sylvester."

"You must call me Krista. May I ask? Are you related to the Duke?" She hoped her question sounded like a polite query.

"My great-grandfather for my sins." Sylvester touched his chest and smiled with great charm. He was accustomed to this question whenever his name was mentioned. "My father is a younger son of a younger son – plenty of social cachet but no money, don't you know!" He laughed.

Krista wanted to jump up and run screaming from the room. Was it her imagination or was he regarding her very closely?

"Now that the civilities are out of the way, take a seat." The abbot gestured towards the free chair in front of his desk. "Would you care for some tea?"

"Thank you, Etienne, but no." Sylvester took a seat, placing the brown-paper package tied with string on his lap. "I cannot become accustomed to drinking that flowery water you enjoy."

"Perhaps I should leave you gentlemen alone," Krista said. "I have taken up a great deal of the abbot's time this morning." She made to stand.

"No, no." Sylvester Stowe-Grenville waved one long-fingered hand lazily. "Do not allow me to run you off, I beg of you. Poor Etienne is being driven almost insane by my constant jumping in and out of his room with my problems. I could not bear it if I ran off such a charming young lady."

Krista sat back down.

"Well, then," said the abbot, "may I know what has driven you to my door this time, Sylvester – unless of course the matter is of a delicate nature?"

"I found this package while sorting through my predecessor's paperwork." Sylvester tapped the parcel on his lap. "It contains what appears to be letters in German. I don't know what I need to do about them and wondered if one of your monks could translate them for me."

"German!" The abbot laughed softly. "The Lord really does provide." He gestured towards Krista. "This young lady would have no problem translating the documents for you."

"I say – really? That would be too marvellous for words. Would you mind awfully, Krista?"

"I can certainly give you a general overview of what the letters say ..." She couldn't deny her knowledge of German, having admitted it to the abbot who was smiling benignly at her.

"Might I suggest you take this young lady to your study, Sylvester?" The abbot stood. He had matters he needed to attend to. "You can offer her a pot of coffee while she works. He may be a charming rogue, Krista, but I assure you he will be everything gentlemanly. You need have no fear being alone with him. He has a small household staff in residence."

"Capital idea." Sylvester stood. "If you don't mind, Krista?"

"I have nowhere I need to be urgently." Krista gathered her belongings before standing. This was certainly turning out to be an interesting day off to say the least.

"You may let Brother Gaston know when you need your coat, Krista," the abbot said, walking them to the door. "If you find yourself in need of a taste of home again – do knock – we will be delighted to have you join us in our small chapel – no need to stand in the rain."

"Thank you, monseigneur. You have been very kind."

"It was a pleasure, my dear."

Krista followed Sylvester into the hallway.

"Come." Sylvester took her elbow as the door closed at their backs. "I'll have Mrs Everly brew up a pot of coffee."

He practically hauled her out of the stable block,

along the pathways that bordered the tilled ground and well-tended patches of garden to the back door of the large three-storey house standing majestically against the grey sky.

"Allow me to give you a little background on my situation." Sylvester walked through the back door as he spoke. "I recently inherited this …" he waved his hand around his head in a circle, "I don't really know what to call it – a house – a living? Anyway, an establishment and a barony. It was a delightful surprise but I am now frantically trying to tie up the loose ends of my predecessor."

They walked up a flight of stairs and down a long dark hallway. When they arrived at a closed door which she presumed led to the kitchen, Sylvester opened it and shouted aloud for a pot of coffee to be served in his study. He didn't wait for a response, simply closed the door and continued walking.

"Since we were introduced by the good abbot, I feel I may be candid with you." Sylvester opened a door, reaching in to turn on the electric light. "I know I should be thrilled and delighted to inherit a baronetcy but I am floundering. Have you ever heard of a London residence with a monastery in the back garden?"

They entered the booklined room. Krista suppressed a shudder. It was dark and dismal in spite of the electric light hanging from the ceiling. The roaring fire in the handsome marble fireplace didn't appear to heat the room.

He threw the parcel onto a heavy desk in front of the

long wide windows, walked over to the glowing fire and kicked the logs.

She joined him by the fire.

"Tell me a little about yourself, Krista." Sylvester held his hands out to the fire. "It was quite a surprise to see old Etienne entertaining such an attractive female."

She was saved from having to answer by a brisk knock on the study door.

"Come in!" Sylvester turned to Krista. "That will be old Everly. You will see – even the servants here are dour."

They stood warming themselves by the fire while a tall thin man dressed in faded black carried an occasional table into the room. He didn't smile or speak as he organised the table in front of the fire, then pulled two wooden chairs which had been standing against one wall of the room to the table.

"I will return with the coffee momentarily," he said.

Bowing his head briefly, he left the room.

"Old Everly does not approve of me." Sylvester's laugh was a trifle bitter.

Krista didn't know what to do or say. It was an exceedingly strange situation to find herself in.

They remained standing in front of the fire until Everly returned and began arranging a silver coffee service and delicate porcelain on the small table.

"Come join me, Krista," Sylvester said when the servant had left the room. "How do you take your coffee?"

"Black, please." She sat in one of the chairs.

"I know who you are." Sylvester held a coffee cup and saucer across the table to her. "It has been driving me wild since we were first introduced."

"I beg your pardon?" Krista took the cup and saucer from his hand, proud when the delicate porcelain didn't rattle. She stared into Sylvester's pale-blue eyes while her mind scurried.

"You are the mystery female who caused such ructions at Great-grandfather's winter ball." He laughed, showing gleaming white teeth. "Did you know my father and all of the family were called onto the carpet after you left?"

"Really?" In preparation for a fact-finding journey into Germany in the company of Peregrine Fotheringham-Carter and under the command of Captain Waters of the British army, she was ordered to attend a social gala in the upper echelon of British society. Peregrine, Perry to his friends, was born into that society but it was felt Krista should experience a high-society gathering in case she should ever be called upon to speak with knowledge of the society she would claim to belong to while on her mission. Lady Winchester, a close childhood friend of her natural mother's – upon being consulted – decided that the winter ball at the Duke of Stowe-Grenville's country estate in Bishop Stortford would be an ideal venue for their purpose.

So it was that Krista, in the company of Lia, Captain Caulfield, Lord and Lady Winchester and family attended one of the most distinguished social events of the season. The event had the secondary purpose of allowing her to view her mother's family home and meet her natural mother's family. The event would have passed without incident except for the fact that the old duke had her removed from the ballroom in order to demand answers as to the reason she so resembled members of his family – answers she refused to give.

"Yes, indeed, your appearance at the ball really put the cat among the pigeons. The ducal residence shook while Great-grandfather roared his demand for explanations. One could not help overhearing the old man's demand for your natural parent to step forward." He waited, hoping she would supply him with some information. He sipped his coffee, looking over the rim of his cup at the elegant, calm young woman sitting across from him. She really was a beauty.

"I understood you invited me here to translate some documents." Krista sipped the coffee, thrilled to discover it was well brewed and not the brown dishwater she'd been expecting. It helped to calm her nerves.

"Come now!" Sylvester gave her one of his charming smiles. "Are you really going to sit there and deny me an answer to the questions that have been keeping my cousins and me entertained for simply ages?"

"Sylvester," she leaned forward, putting her cup onto its saucer, "you asked me here to translate some documents, not provide entertainment."

"You are being most unkind." He stared at her, unable to believe she was not willing to satisfy his curiosity. What was the big mystery? He waited, willing her to explain what it was about her that had so upset the head of his family. When she simply stared back, he relented. "Very well, we will table that discussion for the moment but don't for a minute expect me to let it lie now that I have met you."

He jumped to his feet, startling her. Walking over, he grabbed the package from the desk, returning to almost throw it at her.

"The light here is probably the best in the room. If you wouldn't mind?"

He threw himself into his chair, glaring at her. How dare she deny him? Who did she think she was?

She ignored him, opening the package on the table and reading the top letter – a letter between friends. Her heart sank as she continued to read through the stack, all the time conscious of his displeasure. Well, so be it. She hadn't asked to come here. She was doing him a favour. The letters appeared to be applications for positions on the baron's estate. Was the baron a landowner? The more she read, the deeper her frown. There was something not quite right about the letters of application. She couldn't put her finger on what was bothering her about the correspondence. Had her relationship with Captain Waters and Perry caused her to see intrigue everywhere? The letters seemed to be applications on first glance but surely one didn't mention the height of the leeks one grew or the composition of the soil one used in an application? There was something about the letters that made her skin itch. Was she seeing what was not there? What on earth should she do? Surely a member of the Stowe-

Grenville family could not be a spy? She had to say something – but could she trust this man?

"If I might ask ..." Krista looked directly at him. "Baron, are you a landowner?" She pointed to the papers. "I ask because these appear to be applications for positions on a large country estate."

"To my knowledge my unexpected inheritance did not turn me into a member of the landed gentry." Sylvester stared. "I am still discovering just what I have inherited but I assure you I would have noticed if a large country estate was included in Baron Sturbridge's legacy."

"Baron ..."

"Sylvester, please. I have only recently inherited. I am uncomfortable being addressed by a title. I keep looking over my shoulder to see who is being addressed."

"Sylvester," Krista gulped and unconsciously straightened in the chair, "were you on close terms with your predecessor? I ask for a reason."

"Not at all. I never knew the man. I inherited the estate quite suddenly from a relative on my maternal side of the family. It came as quite a shock to me. I am still trying to learn my responsibilities."

"I may very well be seeing something that is not there, but ..." Krista wished herself miles away. "The letters, including a cover letter from what appears to be a close friend of the previous Baron Sturbridge, appear on the surface to be letters of application. They are from carpenters, gardeners, stable masters, even a butler, but something about them is not quite what it seems. I am no expert but there are details included in each letter that appear to my eyes to be excessive and unnecessary information about each person's job skills, for want of a better word."

"I am no expert in writing or indeed receiving letters of application." Sylvester wondered what this young woman was trying so hard not to say. "But wouldn't one supply detailed information about the skills brought to the position he or she sought?"

"I do apologise if I seem alarmist. I believe the letters contain some sort of coded messages." She ignored his shocked gasp. "There is simply no need," she put a hand to her chest, "in my opinion to state how tall one's vegetables grow or the height of the horses one tends. There is simply something not at all as it should be with these letters." She waved towards the documents sitting so innocently on the tabletop.

"Is anything about this dashed inheritance going to be good news?" He shoved his fingers through his hair. "What on earth am I supposed to do about all of this?" He flung himself back in his chair, sighing deeply.

Chapter 3

Krista walked along the wet, muddy London streets, her chin buried in her scarf. It had given her such joy to spend the early morning hours speaking French with the abbot. And croissants – a taste of home – wonderful! There were so many things she missed about the village of Metz – as it was – not as it was becoming. She had not appreciated how difficult it was to speak a language not your own constantly. Perhaps she could find French friends to spend time with? It was something worth thinking about.

She wished the libraries opened on Sunday. She would have somewhere to sit out of the rain that continued to fall. She didn't read a great many books.

She found reading in English a great deal of effort. How she longed to find books written in French – reading them would relax her mind. She continued to trundle along the wide streets, window-shopping as she went. She would never be able to afford anything from the shops in Regent's Street but she could look.

She had refused Sylvester Stowe-Grenville's offer to wait out the rain in his house. A feeling of disapproval seemed to almost ooze out of the very walls of that dark mausoleum. When he had offered lunch, she'd had to fight to hide her horror at the very suggestion. The place and the obviously resentful man servant would give anyone indigestion.

Should she have told him about her parents? Was there a correct way to introduce yourself as the base-born child of his father's deceased sister? Why was she determined to keep the news of her birth secret? She was the innocent in all of this.

Her feet kicked at the puddles of rainwater dotting the streets under her feet. What would he do about those letters she'd translated for him? He could of course just throw them to one side and ignore them. She felt strongly that, with the state of the world at the moment, someone should be made aware of their content. She had no contact details for the Grey Man, Mr Brown. Surely something of that nature should be brought to his attention?

She continued to walk the streets, the rain soaking into her coat adding to the weight of the garment. She felt alone and lonely, her mind circling around problems that really had nothing to do with her.

"*Oh, là là,*" she muttered under her breath, "you are having a fine time feeling sorry for yourself. You should be grateful for all your blessings. Lia Caulfield did not have to give you a fine roof over your head, feed you and pay you for the little you do. You are being an ungrateful so-and-so, Krista Lestrange." In the middle of her lecture to herself, she saw a big red bus coming and ran towards the bus stop. She needed to get out of the rain and dry off. She put her hand out to signal to the driver. She climbed aboard the bus, falling into the first free seat she came to.

"Wet enough for you, love?" the bus conductor quipped when he was taking her fare. "Fine weather for bloomin' ducks out there." He used the handle on the side of the ticket machine strapped around his neck and falling onto his stomach to run off her ticket. He didn't wait for a response but walked along the bus calling, "*Fares, please, fares!*"

Krista took her muddy boots off, leaving them to one side of the door. She used her key to open the door and stepped into the hallway, her stocking feet almost curling at the chill from the tiles.

"*Krista!*" David shouted from the top of the stairs. He was leaning over the banister, shouting down the stairwell. "*I can't find my giraffe! I want to take my zoo with me to Harry's house!*"

"*You may not take the zoo with you, David!*" Lia yelled from the twins' playroom.

Edward appeared beside his twin. "*Mama cannot find our toys, Krista! Where did you put them?*"

"I'll be up in just a minute." Krista hurried towards the back of the house. She needed to hang her coat up to dry.

"Give us a hand, would you, Krista?" Peggy said as soon as Krista stepped into the kitchen.

"I will in a while, Peggy." Krista pulled a kitchen chair in front of the range, making sure it was out of Peggy's way. She draped her coat over the back of the chair. "Lia needs help with the boys then I will be down to help you."

"Did you get anything to eat?" Peggy asked. "I put a plate in the warming oven for you."

"I am fine for the moment, thank you."

Krista hurried through the kitchen, out to the hall and up the stairs. She stopped briefly in her room to push her cold feet into her fleece-lined leather slippers.

"Now," she said, standing in the open door of the twin's playroom, "what is it you are looking for?"

"If you take care of them, Krista," Lia walked past, "I'll finish getting ready."

Krista spent time packing the small knapsacks she had bought the twins as a Christmas gift. She had to be firm with them. They wanted to take the entire contents of the playroom with them, it seemed. Then she took the boys to the kitchen. They played with their cars on the kitchen table while Krista gave Peggy a hand with the many little chores involved in cleaning up after the family's Sunday lunch. The two young women worked silently, each wanting to get the chore finished, and conscious of the two boys – they were capable of repeating everything they heard – so it was best to simply tend to the chores and not converse.

"Boys, bring your toys upstairs to the playroom." Krista took off the apron she had been wearing to protect her clothes. "Come along, boys!"

She helped the boys pick up their little cars and almost pushed them in front of her out of the kitchen. They went upstairs to the playroom.

Krista stood in the doorway. "I will be in the bathroom if you need me. Your mother will be along shortly. Play quietly for a moment and try and remain clean and tidy – please!"

"Thank you, Krista." Lia had come up the stairs without Krista noticing. She touched Krista's shoulder gently. "I will take over now." She stepped into the playroom.

Krista went to her own room. She listened to the sound of the boys being prepared for their visit to one of Lia's friends. Peggy should be leaving soon. She would be glad of the chance to sit and think about all that had happened that morning. When she heard the excited boys shouting goodbye to her she left her bedroom.

She used the bathroom, cleaning herself up before running down the stairs. Peggy had left. She set a place at the kitchen table for herself before taking her meal from the warming oven. Peggy had left everything spotlessly clean. She sighed deeply as she stared at the heaped plate of roast beef and Yorkshire pudding. Was it any wonder the French referred to the English as "roast beef"?

While eating her meal, she listened to a music programme on the wireless. The quiet house was a balm to her soul. What a morning it had been! Would she dare return to the monastery? The abbot had invited her and she so enjoyed the sound of male voices raised in prayer. She sighed deeply but gave an unconscious Gallic shrug. She would see.

She tidied up after her meal before pulling the table with the typewriting machines on top into the kitchen. She would get some practice in while she had the place to herself. The twins thought the typewriter machines were the most amazing toys – and one each to their little minds. They had to be wrestled away from the keys on a regular basis.

She rolled a sheet of blank paper into the machine, checked the black-and-red fabric ribbon was tight and began. A-S-D-F-G-F space. Her fingers flew across the keys practising the drills they had learned in class. Without conscious thought her fingers began to type the words that had bothered her from the letters she had translated that morning. She couldn't forget the details that had been given in what were supposed to be job applications. Were they code? Was she seeing intrigue where none existed? While her mind worried and wondered she continued to type the phrases that had bothered her.

In the weeks that followed Krista continued to attend school, where she was making friends. She returned several times to the monastery. There was no sign of the abbot or Sylvester Stowe-Grenville but she was allowed sit in the small chapel and revel in the glorious music.

"Do you not wish they would turn off that dreadful wireless?" Marina Latham, a vivacious blonde, groaned, her brown eyes glaring at the offending object.

Krista jerked her attention away from the words of doom pouring from the wireless. The students were taking a short break in the room set aside for their use. The dining room of the Huxley house had been set up as a breakroom for them. A large silver tea urn sat on the sideboard, heavy white delft cups and saucers stacked nearby for student use. The table sat twenty. A wireless in a handsome cabinet was set into one corner of the room.

"My dad says we're heading towards war." Vicky Nixon, a redheaded dynamo, said. Her green eyes, shaded by thick lashes, roamed around the people at the table. "He says that Mr Hitler can't be trusted."

"Please, Vicky," Marina sniffed, "your father sweeps the streets for the council. What on earth would he know?"

"My dad fought in the Great War and was gassed!" Vicky pushed up the sleeves of her tatty jumper. No one spoke badly of her dad while she was around.

"Ladies, please," Krista put in, "we only have a short break. Let us have a cup of tea in peace."

"I have an interview at a solicitor's office next week," Marina said from her place to the right of Krista. "My father arranged it. He believes it will be a good starting position for me."

"It's well for some people," Vicky said from her seat to Krista's left.

Krista looked at the two girls who had befriended her. They made an unlikely pair but they had been a great help to her as she struggled to fit in with the other students. At the start of the school year the students had been sorted into groups by family name. Lia Caulfield was in a different group from Krista. She could have been very lonely but these two young women had made it their business to help her fit in. She was grateful to them both.

"What are you going to do when we are finished up here, Krista?" Vicky asked.

"With the news coming out of Europe I believe our options will be limited." Krista sighed.

"I have no wish to hear that kind of talk from you, Krista Lestrange!" Marina snapped. "I hear quite enough of that from that dreadful wireless." She searched for her cigarettes in the pocket of her black skirt. "We are young and attractive. This is our time to have fun. Honestly, I do not know why I keep company with the pair of you – doomsayers, both of you."

"It must be nice to live in your fairyland." Vicky's green eyes glared.

"I don't know what I'm going to do," Krista said, ignoring the flare-up between the two women. It was nothing new. The news from Europe was frightening. Hitler was on the march. Czechoslovakia was being torn apart. Germany had annexed one portion of that country in the final months of 1938. Now, in the month of March, Poland and Hungary were nibbling on the borders of Czechoslovakia.

"I have heard that the Wrens are being reformed," Vicky leaned in to say. "My dad says they were something to see in the Great War. He has nothing but praise for them. If we have a choice in what we do – the Wrens would be my preference."

"You might well be in with a chance, Vicky." Krista had heard all about the troubles and needs of the Wrens – the WRNS – from the woman she thought of as her guardian, Violet Andrews. The woman was at the heart of the drive to re-establish them. "I have heard they are taking applications from women who will be prepared to step up at a moment's notice." She bit her lip. "However, at the moment they are only employing volunteers. To my knowledge, no mention of a wage has been established." She knew that Vicky, like herself, could not afford to work for nothing.

"My dad says we women will be called up," Vicky said.

"Nonsense!" Marina curled her scarlet-painted lips around her cigarette.

"Come on, ladies, let's be having yeh!" Gertie, the older woman who kept things moving at the school, walked into the break room. "Get back to your desks. Time for the next lot."

There was a general scramble as the students pushed their chairs back under the table and left their used cups on the sideboard as they left the room.

***

Krista ran through the back streets of London, her knapsack with her schoolbooks and supplies inside bouncing on her back in time with her running footsteps. She had timed this journey to the last minute. She had to arrive at the twins' school gates before the bell went to signal the release of the young pupils. With Mrs Huxley's approval she left the last of her own classes ten minutes ahead of everyone else. She sometimes wished she could stay back as Lia did. The women often lingered after class to enjoy tea and a chat at a nearby tearoom. But she was being paid to tend to the twins. Leaving the boys to school and collecting them was part of her duties.

"Look at you two!" Krista laughed at the untidy little boys running towards her with yells of delight. Their coats were open, falling off their little shoulders. They dragged their schoolbags along the ground behind them. "Honestly, David, Edward, how on earth do you manage to make such a mess of your uniform every day?" She attempted to restore order to their rumpled black hair, her busy fingers pulling at their collars and coats. She did up their coats and helped each boy put his schoolbag on his back.

Then, taking a hand of each of them, she began the stroll back to the Caulfield house.

"Imagine the trouble your father would be in if he allowed his uniform to become a mess." The boys' father was a captain in the Royal Navy.

"But Papa is a big boy." David looked up at Krista, his green eyes wide and innocent. "We are little boys," he stated with great satisfaction and a nod of his head.

"Our heads are only little, Krista," Edward, his twin's mirror image, said. "We cannot know everything yet."

They walked along the streets, Krista being entertained by the twin's innocent remarks. She was making a mental list of all she had to do when they reached the house. There would be no time for her to sit and put her feet up. She supposed she wasn't hard done by. Vicky Nixon – for a reduction of her fees – remained behind after the school closed and cleaned the classrooms and hallways. She would then spend time practising her typing on one of the school's typewriters. Thanks to Lia, Krista had her own typewriter to practise on when the boys were asleep. Her days were busy from the time she opened her eyes until she went to bed. Thank goodness for Sundays!

"Wipe your feet carefully, boys, and down to the kitchen," Krista said when they reached home. "Don't take anything off until I get there." She had learned that it was best to tell the boys exactly what she wanted them to do. Wilma Acers had almost had a nervous breakdown the first time the twins kicked off their shoes and threw their bags and coats onto her gleaming kitchen floor.

After closing the door, she removed her own haversack. She removed her coat and hung it on the hallway hat-stand. With her haversack in hand, she hurried down to the kitchen where the boys were shouting aloud their return. She laughed softly under her breath. As if anyone could miss the return of the pair.

"Boys, into the mudroom!"

Wilma Acers was preparing a snack for them. Peggy was setting the kitchen table and carrying items from the pantry under the cook's direction.

Krista ushered the two boys towards the mudroom. She needed to remove their coats and shoes and take their lunch boxes from their schoolbags. "Put your inside shoes on, boys," she said as she removed their school shoes. She sighed at the state of the black leather shoes. It was her job to remove the dirt and scuff marks, polishing the shoes until they shone, ready for the next day.

"You had a telephone call when you were out, Krista!" Peggy called towards where Krista was washing the boys' hands and faces at the kitchen sink.

"Not another one!" Krista pinched David's nose gently when he giggled at her obvious dismay.

"No, it wasn't one of those Hurray Henrys telephoning," Peggy was quick to assure her.

"Thank goodness." The young men on the course with Perry had made nuisances of themselves, telephoning the house to speak with her. "Who was trying to contact me?"

"It was Miss Andrews. She knew you were at school but wanted to leave a message for you. She said she would visit you this evening. I didn't think you had any other plans. Was that all right?"

"That's fine." Krista escorted the boys to the table.

"It will be good to see her. Did she mention a time?" She helped each boy onto his seat, passing each the glass of fresh milk Peggy poured for them.

"I told her what time our pair of troublemakers go to bed." Peggy laughed.

"Are we the troublemakers?" Edward, a milk moustache on his face, asked.

"We are not troublemakers," David objected. "Are we, Krista?"

"I cannot imagine who Peggy is referring to." Krista smiled down at the two little mischief-makers.

Chapter 4

"It is so good to see you, Miss Andrews." Krista greeted the woman who had been her teacher of English while they lived in France. The woman who had assisted her in her escape from France and who had done everything in her power to help her settle into her new life.

"Violet, please. There is no need for us to stand on ceremony. I really should apologise, my dear, it is frightfully late to be paying a call." Violet Andrews passed her hat and coat to the young girl she had come to think of as her ward. "I wanted to be sure it was past the boys' bedtime so we would have a chance to talk in peace."

"Come into the kitchen." Krista hung Violet's coat and hat on the hall stand before leading the way into the kitchen. "It is the warmest room in the house. And our voices won't carry up the hallway. The boys are sound asleep. I checked." She laughed. "Lia is not at home. She has been spending a great deal of time with ladies from the Women's Institute. From what she tells me the women are trying to form a plan of action if the unthinkable should happen and war comes. Peggy has a date with an admirer so we have the kitchen to ourselves."

"I consider myself rather fortunate to find you at home on a Friday evening. I thought you might be out with an admirer yourself." Violet followed Krista into the kitchen. "I heard that the telephone lines were burning from the number of times the young bucks in Perry's class have telephoned this house seeking your attention."

"Yes, indeed." Krista laughed loudly, her blue eyes sparkling as she indicated the two easy chairs she had pulled into the kitchen and put in front of the range. "They were all frightfully keen on spending time with me until I mentioned the fee I would demand for my individual time and attention."

"Krista, you didn't?" Violet dropped into one of the easy chairs, staring at the younger woman in horror. "What on earth would make you do such a thing – your reputation will be in tatters."

"Those young men – each and every one of them – wished to use me to practise their language skills." She waved a hand in the air when Violet looked like objecting. "I daresay the pleasure of my company would have been a bonus. I am not unattractive. But it was my language skills they wanted – since that is one of my few marketable skills – and why should they receive the benefit of my knowledge for free?"

"That is rather a unique way of looking at things." Violet stared up at Krista, trying not to allow her mouth to fall open.

"Did you not charge for teaching English to the people of Metz?"

"Hoist on my own petard, by golly!" Violet had indeed charged the people of Metz for English lessons. It was one way of augmenting her rather meagre income.

"Those young men all have trust funds. They have no idea of the difficulties involved in earning a living for oneself. They were all horrified when I suggested I should charge them." She shrugged, not really bothered by the attitude of people she didn't know and would never normally cross paths with. She turned in a circle, looking around the kitchen for a moment. "I don't know what to offer you. We have tea, coffee, hot chocolate or something stronger."

"I would enjoy a hot chocolate, thank you." Violet Andrews allowed the subject to drop. What could she say after all? "I am sorry I haven't been to see you lately. We have been so frantically busy." Violet and a group of her cronies from their time in the Wrens in the Great War were frantically working behind the scenes to resurrect the women's naval service in time for what they considered the coming conflict.

"Strangely, we were speaking about the Wrens at

school today." Krista was taking the items she needed to make hot chocolate from the pantry. "One of the women in my class wishes to join but like myself it is not possible for her to work for nothing. She needs to contribute to her family's household expenses. Vicky Nixon would be an ideal candidate for the Wrens. Will the Admiralty pay a wage if you succeed in re-establishing it?"

"Would that I could answer your question!" Violet dropped her weary head onto the back of her chair. "We are receiving hundreds if not thousands of written applications. We have women who have left their homes and families to answer the call. We are working hard to put rules and regulations in place. It is dreadfully difficult but we will prevail."

"Do you wish me to become a Wren?" Krista asked the question over her shoulder while putting milk to warm on the range top.

"My dear ..." Violet felt desperately sorry for what she had to say. "Your background would never stand up to the investigation the Navy insists on for all women wishing to be Wrens." It was heart-breaking that this child should be penalised for the perceived sins of her parents.

"I had wondered," Krista said simply as she stirred grated chocolate into the heating milk. She didn't like to think of some faceless strangers enquiring into her life for the purpose of allowing her to join the Wrens. It was bad enough that she could almost feel the Grey Man breathing down her neck.

"There are agencies with letters for names springing

up all over London, sticking their noses into matters that don't concern them it would appear to me." Violet sighed.

Krista poured the chocolate into the two mugs she had close to hand. She carried the mugs over to the chairs and, after passing one to Violet, took her seat across the range from the other woman.

Violet sipped her chocolate. "Mrs Huxley speaks very highly of you, as regards your studies."

"That is kind of her. I have been most fortunate. Lea bought two typewriting machines for our use. They have helped greatly in increasing our speed and accuracy while typing. The dreaded squiggles for our shorthand have finally begun to make sense. Lia and I set each other examinations when we have spare time of an evening. It has helped enormously in improving our skills."

"Yes, Mrs Huxley did mention that you two are among her brightest students." Violet kept in touch with Annora Huxley – the woman was a past Wren after all. When the Admiralty finally opened their coffers – as they must – the Wrens could offer a wage packet to women of the right social class who could not afford to offer their services for free. The Wrens would need all of the trained shorthand typists they could attract to their service. "Do you have any plans for when you complete the course? You will have a much needed skill and your English language has improved enormously. You are ready to step out into the world."

"That is a terrifying thought."

"Why terrifying?" Violet asked.

"I have spoken with some of the other young women at Mrs Huxley's school," Krista said slowly. "They all live at home with their families." She sighed deeply. "I have been checking the advertisements in the evening papers. How on earth could I earn enough to live independently? The salaries mentioned for skilled secretaries are a cut above some of the others but I have no experience. Then there are the prices stated for renting a flat. I simply cannot see how I could afford to live alone and support myself."

"You have a great deal of experience in the hotel trade." Violet had been horrified to find the daughter of her dear friend Lady Constance Stowe-Grenville being used as unpaid labour by the family she'd been entrusted to, after her parents had been killed in a car accident when she was just a babe in arms.

"When I first ran away from the Auberge du Ville in Metz I had no fears. I thought I would find a position in a reputable hotel and make a life for myself." She grimaced to remember that innocent girl. It all seemed such a long time ago now yet it wasn't even a full year since she had fled. "After all, most hotel positions are live-in. I would have a roof over my head, food to eat that was prepared for me by someone else and best of all a salary that would be mine alone."

"What changed your mind?" Violet asked. "I can see by your face that someone or something did."

"I mentioned my idea to Mrs Huxley..."

"And ..."

"She took me to one side," Krista said slowly. "She regaled me with horror stories concerning some of her past pupils and men who bothered the young women who worked at some rather famous hotels. It was very revealing." She gave a Gallic shrug. "I had not realised how much I was protected by the men I thought of as my brothers." She shoved her hands through her hair. "Yes, I slept with a chair under my doorknob – but I knew if I screamed someone would come running." There was no need to make mention of her last day at the *auberge* when the man she thought was her father offered a young man she detested the freedom of her body.

"My dear ..."

"While I have been living here I have come to realise how much I do not know about life."

"I have no words of wisdom to offer you, I am afraid." Violet felt very inadequate. She was old enough to be Krista's mother yet she had no knowledge which could be useful in this situation. "I can make enquiries, I suppose. I do know rather vaguely that there are hostels available to young women. There are also private homes that take in young women of good character. Perhaps something of that nature could be of some use to you?"

"I think my best option is to stay where I am for the moment." Krista smiled. "Peggy is teaching me how to take care of my own needs. Mrs Acers insists on teaching me how to prepare simple dishes."

"You are ahead of me therefore." Violet smiled. "I am incapable of preparing a simple meal. I am fortunate in that I have been able to pay for someone else to take care of the house and prepare my meals."

"That is indeed fortunate."

Krista stood, her empty mug in hand. She took the mug Violet held out and with quick practised moves rinsed out both mugs and left them on the draining board. She sat down again opposite Violet.

"Tell me, have you heard anything more from Sylvester Stowe-Grenville?" Violet wanted to change the subject. Krista had written to her about her visit to the monastery and its many surprises. "I have spoken with my friend Abigail, Lady Winchester, about him – she knows that family rather better than myself – she informs me that Sylvester's inheritance is the talk of the family. By the way, he is your first cousin. His father is indeed one of your mother's brothers."

"I have been back to the monastery several times. I have listened to the music but seen neither the Abbot nor Stowe-Grenville. Excuse me a moment." Krista thought she heard the sound of the hall door being opened.

She stood up and quickly walked over and opened the kitchen door. One could never truly relax with two active boys out of sight.

"Krista," Lia appeared, looking distraught, "be a dear and make me some hot chocolate. I am going to fetch the brandy. I need something to warm me and something to help me sleep. I have passed an evening that would try the patience of a saint."

***

"You sound distressed, Lia dear," Violet said when Lia appeared in the kitchen clutching a bottle of brandy in one white-knuckled fist.

Krista was busy preparing more hot chocolate for all.

"Violet, you are still here?" Lia had been told about Violet's planned visit. "I sincerely hope you've been having a more pleasant time than I have."

"I have indeed, thank you. But you, Lia, what has happened? I recognise the signs of someone ready to beat their own head off a wall."

"Committees!" Lia pulled at her hair dramatically. "Who ever invented committees! We have spent the entire evening speaking in circles and achieving nothing as far as I am concerned. I have no wish to knit socks and balaclavas," she said through gritted teeth.

"Do sit down, Lia." Krista was grating chocolate. "As Mrs Acers would say 'you are making the place look untidy'."

"I apologise. I have spent an evening being told of all of the things I cannot do because I am the mother of young children. I want to be involved in what is going on in the world. When Mrs Waverly offered me knitting needles and wool it was all that I could do not to shove the offending items down that dear lady's throat!"

"Did you not tell this Mrs Waverly that you are unable to knit?" Krista added the grated chocolate to the pot of warm milk on the range top.

"Oh, I did indeed state my inability to knit. The dear woman offered to teach me."

Violet began to laugh, unable to hide her amusement

at seeing another woman become as frustrated as she herself became with some of the stuffy rules and regulations she had to contend with on an almost daily basis. She had often felt like beating some of the men of the different ministries and those of the Admiralty over the head.

"You may well laugh, Violet Andrews." Lia accepted a mug of well-doctored chocolate from Krista's hand. She held the mug to her nose for a moment, inhaling the welcome scent of the brandy Krista had added to the warm drink. "But if what I am experiencing is anything to go by – this country of ours is in a great deal of trouble."

Chapter 5

May 1939
Mrs Huxley's school

"Krista, I love your coat and hat – so dashing!" Marina Latham rubbed manicured hands down the sleeve of Krista's red coat.

"Honestly, Marina!" Vicky Nixon glared. "Her coat – is that really what we should be speaking about?"

The three young women formed part of a group waiting in the hallway of Mrs Huxley's house. They were waiting for the results of their exams, a reference and a final brief meeting with Mrs Huxley before they left the school forever.

"I suppose I could mention how dashing I think her navy slacks to be but the coat is eye-catching." Marina threw her blonde hair over her shoulder and turned her back on Vicky, checking to see how much the snaking line of young women had moved. She had matters to attend to.

"Honestly, Marina, you are the giddy limit." Vicky's green eyes were positively flashing.

"I am going to miss you two and your squabbling." Krista grabbed each woman by the elbow and pulled them along with the movement of the line.

"Well, really, Krista," Vicky grumbled, "the world is going to seed around us and all this one," she jerked her chin towards Marina, "can think about is fashion." She threw her hands in the air. "They are putting Anderson shelters all along our street. My parents are crying with relief that my brothers are too young to be conscripted and Marina wants to discuss fashion."

"The world cannot stop because some ugly little man in Germany thinks he can press us all beneath his jackboots." Marina's brown eyes narrowed as she glared at the slow-moving line.

"Have you put in your application to the Wrens, Vicky?" Krista said, ignoring Marina's words. Vicky was frightened. She wasn't the only one. Hitler had started his march across Europe as everyone had feared. The news from the wireless was distressing. Britain was gearing up for war. Groups of workers could be seen all over London installing Anderson shelters into back gardens. Basements were being cleared out in preparation – for what no one knew or understood – not really. How could you prepare for the unthinkable?

"My dad suggested I wait to get the results of my test

and my reference before I apply." Vicky was almost bouncing on her heels. The thought of joining the Navy – her – a girl – it was beyond exciting. "Dad said I could refer to my exam results when I apply. He thinks it will give me a chance over all of the other women applying."

The Wrens had been officially reinstated in April.

"I will keep my fingers crossed for you." Krista hoped Vicky would be accepted but she had her doubts. Violet Andrews had been so excited when the Wrens were once more officially a force that she had regaled the members of the Caulfield household with a list of the requirements the Wrens would look for in their women. It had sounded to Krista – who had listened carefully – that the Wrens were to be selected from only the upper and middle-class echelons of British society. There had been no mention made of young women from Vicky's working-class background.

"They don't even have a uniform yet!" Marina snapped. "I have no wish to join the forces. If there should come a time when I must – I will insist on seeing the uniform before I sign on the dotted line." She sniffed.

"Good for you, Marina." Grace Lucas called over her shoulder. "One must uphold one's standards after all."

"Don't …" Krista grabbed Vicky by the arm when she began to step forward. "The last thing we need is fisticuffs in the hallway."

"Miss Lestrange –" Annora Huxley sat behind her heavy desk, a desk covered in brown envelopes and typewritten pages, staring at the young woman standing so proudly before her. "I have had several requests for your services." The school received notices of vacancies from various business concerns around London. Each new class had the option of several openings to consider. This year, however – she stifled a sigh. She'd been sighing heavily all morning. What was to become of her latest graduates? What sort of world would they be walking into?

"I beg your pardon?" Krista was confused.

"You are legally a British subject." Annora had known this young woman's mother by sight. They had both served in the head offices of the WRNS during the Great War. The resemblance to her mother was striking – she even stood and walked like her mother. Lady Constance had been a familiar figure striding through the halls of power. "You have a British passport and your papers are in order. I checked these very carefully."

"Yes, Mrs Huxley." What was she supposed to say?

"Your exam results were excellent." She held out a sheet of typed paper, waiting until Krista took it from her hand. "I have composed a reference for you." She picked up one of the brown envelopes from her desk and held it out. "The different government services and several international businesses have been baying for your services." She picked up a large well-stuffed brown envelope and held it out towards Krista. "You have no experience as a secretary obviously. However, you can name your price. It is your language skills that are much sought after. Study the papers in that envelope and choose wisely."

"Thank you, Mrs Huxley." Krista's head was in a spin. What on earth was in the envelope?

"I wish you all the very best for the future, Miss Lestrange." Annora Huxley waved a hand. "Send in the next girl, please."

"Goodbye and thank you, Mrs Huxley." Krista clutched the papers to her chest and walked out of the room.

She held the door open for the next young woman who happened to be Vicky. Marina had already had her interview.

"Vicky ..." Marina looked at Krista, unsure how to continue.

It was obvious Vicky had received bad news from Mrs Huxley but what could it be? Vicky had surely passed all of her exams. She had worked harder than anyone else in the class, for goodness' sake!

The three young women were sitting around a table in the local Lyon's tearoom. They had agreed to a final meeting before they parted to go on with their separate lives. They had been served tea and cakes and could now speak freely.

"Vicky, something has upset you. Do you want to tell us about it?" Krista reached for her teacup.

"*It is not fair!*" Vicky almost hissed. She stared at her companions with moist green eyes. "Krista is foreign but she sounds like someone off the wireless. Marina, you talk with a plum in your mouth." She stared almost accusingly at the other two.

"Does any of that matter?" Marina put one of the cream cakes on her side plate. "We three are friends, are we not?"

"Our differences have always been there, Vicky." Krista wiped her mouth with her napkin. "Why mention them now?"

"Mrs Huxley advised me not to apply to the Wrens ..." Vicky fought the sobs that had been sitting under her ribs since the interview with Mrs Huxley.

"But that is your dream!" Krista said.

"Why on earth would the woman say something of that nature?" Marina stared, shocked. "Surely you would be perfect for the Wrens. You even live in Greenwich by the Maritime Museum. The Navy is almost in your blood."

"It seems every time I open my mouth I announce my working-class background," Vicky whispered.

"I had not taken Mrs Huxley for a snob," Marina said.

Krista felt terrible for her friend but she had suspected something of this nature would happen.

"I have been given," Vicky tapped the large brown envelope on the table in front of her. "situations vacant in builder's yards – transport companies – and several others to which I am apparently well suited."

"In my opinion," Marina said, "that is rubbish. Surely we have moved on from outdated ideas of class. We will all bleed red when war comes as everyone says it must."

"That is rather profound from you, Marina," Krista said. "I am impressed."

"*It is not fair*," Vicky said. "I am being judged not by my skills – which are excellent, by the way – but by the way I sound and look. I can do nothing about my accent and place in life. That is just an accident of birth."

"I cannot believe that Mrs Huxley advised you to give up on your dream," Marina said. "The woman was a Wren herself, for goodness' sake!"

"Mrs Huxley was everything that is kind." Vicky sighed. "She tried to approach the subject delicately. She told me that the Wrens do not yet have a uniform. They will be wearing their own garments until a uniform is decided upon." She pulled at the unravelling cuff of her old knitted cardigan. "She waltzed around the subject but in essence she advised that I would be out of my class and perhaps the subject of some amusement for the other women if I did happen to be taken on by the Wrens – which she doubted."

"I am sorry, Vicky." Krista laid one hand over the clenched fist of her friend. "I too cannot apply to any of the services. I am foreign as you have said. One must have two parents born in Britain to be suitable for service apparently."

"What were you offered, Krista?" Marina was uncomfortable at the realisation that her birth alone gave her opportunities that were denied to her two companions. She had never been more aware of her privileges.

"I do not know." Krista shrugged. "I have not looked."

"Why not?" Marina and Vicky asked together.

"I had not planned to move from my present position."

"You cannot remain in a low-paid position now that you have skills to offer," Marina objected.

"Why would you wish to remain as a type of nanny to young boys when you can enter the work force with skills that are much in demand?" Vicky stared at Krista, forgetting her own disappointments for a moment.

"Unlike you two," Krista smiled sadly, "I have no home to go to."

"I say!" Marina gulped.

"I am sorry." Vicky reached over and squeezed Krista's shoulder. "I had given no thought to your living arrangements."

"You haven't said, Marina, what positions you have been offered?" Krista didn't want to discuss her own problems. This would perhaps be the last time the three of them could get together. She would rather think of the positive.

"I am rather disappointed with my own selection, to tell the truth." Marina was happy to change the subject.

"Why?" Vicky couldn't imagine Marina was offered situations in rough quarters.

"I had expressed my interest in working for lawyers and professional men," Marina grimaced. "I had visions of being private secretary to some lovely man." She sighed. "Unfortunately, until I actually have some work experience I would be employed as assistant to the private secretary of the head of the firm or some such."

"What happened with that solicitor your father arranged for you to have an interview with?"

"A rather fusty older gentleman with roving eyes

and fingers!" Marina snapped. "Most unsuitable. I am determined to marry a man from the legal community. I believe I can catch the eye of an eligible party if given the chance."

"Marina, I despair of you!" Krista laughed. This was not the first time they had been regaled about Marina's quest for a husband.

"Excuse me," Marina stood, "I must powder my nose."

Vicky waited until Marina was well away from the table, walking towards the ladies' room, before leaning in towards Krista.

"I have never said before ..." Vicky looked around quickly but it seemed they were of no interest to any of the people in Lyons'. "My mother offers lodgement to gentlewomen as do many of our neighbours in Greenwich." She waited a moment for Krista to think about what she had said. "My mother and several others have been approached by the navy with a view to offering lodgement to the young women who sign on as Wrens."

"Vicky, how exciting for you!" Krista didn't immediately understand why Vicky had offered this information. "Does your mother have room for Wrens?"

"I was thinking of your situation." Vicky shrugged, not understanding Krista's excitement.

"But, think about it, Vicky." Krista covered one of Vicky's hands on the table and shook it slightly. "You are not stupid. You have told me you were always head of the class at school."

"What has that to do with anything?" Vicky saw

Marina return from the ladies' room. She didn't want her to know of her home situation.

"What are you discussing?" Marina took her seat her nose freshly powdered, her lipstick without blemish.

"I have been trying to advise Vicky not to despair." Krista had seen Vicky's reaction and understood it. She had never mentioned working in the Auberge du Ville to her companions. "It would appear several of her neighbours in Greenwich have been approached to lodge the young women who will join the Wrens."

"And ..." Marina shared a confused look with Vicky.

"Don't you see?" Krista appealed to the other two. "Vicky could make a study of the young women. She could befriend them and learn to copy their mannerisms. She would have time to turn herself into the perfect Wren. Then, when the Wrens have their uniforms, she can apply and no-one will be any the wiser."

"Are you suggesting that Vicky should 'ape her betters'?" Marina gasped.

"Have either of you read George Bernard Shaw's play *Pygmalion*?" Krista laughed. "One of the main characters – Professor Henry Higgins – turned a barrow girl into a supposed wealthy lady and heaven knows Vicky is no barrow girl!" Krista sat back in her seat and waited.

"That is a work of fiction," Marina objected. "I have seen the play."

"But it has been argued that Professor Higgins is

based on actual people who teach others to speak correctly." Krista shrugged. She leaned forward and fixed her eyes on Vicky. "We are all agreed war is coming. No-one knows when or how but everyone seems to agree it is coming. But you have time, time to work and earn money. You can purchase some very attractive outfits at the better quality stalls in the market. You can practise your diction. Heaven's above, use the wireless and copy how the people on there speak. If you want to be a Wren you have time to turn yourself into the perfect candidate."

"My word, Krista Lestrange, when you dream – you dream outrageously." Marina was intrigued by the suggestion. Vicky was a very attractive young woman. Why shouldn't she try to better her station in life?

"My dad has always said you can do anything you set your mind to." Vicky felt as if Krista had given her a glimpse of a different way of life. Could she do it? She would bloomin' well try! Nothing ventured, nothing gained, after all.

Chapter 6

"Put the kettle on, pet," Claudia Nixon said when her daughter stepped through the back door of their Victorian terraced house. She continued to peel potatoes. She had dinner to prepare for her lady lodgers. "We'll have a cuppa while you tell me about your test results." She had no fear that this daughter of hers had failed. Vicky had always been a bright spark.

Vicky carried her coat and bag into the family room off the kitchen. The large kitchen and the housekeeper's room off the kitchen were the family's private areas, away from the 'best' rooms which were kept pristine for the lady lodgers use only.

Back in the kitchen, she quickly pulled the large

black kettle off the back of the range and onto the hottest part. She took down one of the many teapots arranged by size on a shelf over the range and put it – with a little water from the kettle – onto the range top.

"I thought you would be bouncing off the ceiling when you came home." Claudia put the potatoes into a large pot of salted water then wiped her hands on the apron she wore over her grey woollen skirt and jumper. She was an older version of Vicky – an attractive woman despite the worries and troubles she fought daily. "What's wrong, pet?"

"Oh, Mam!" Vicky dropped into one of the kitchen chairs and her green eyes filled with tears. "Mrs Huxley said my dream of joining the Wrens was a fool's desire." She dropped her head into her hands and wept.

"Oh, pet!" Claudia drew her eldest child to her breast and rocked her gently, all the while keeping her eyes on the kitchen clock. Vicky could not be crying when her brothers came home from school or they would never hear the end of it. "Here," she pressed a tea towel into Vicky's hands. "Wipe your face and sit up straight. I'll make the tea. We have a few minutes before the boys are home."

"I'm sorry, Mam, you have enough to do without me turning into a leaky faucet."

Vicky pressed the cloth to her face. She jumped to her feet and, while her mother made the tea, began taking cups and saucers from the Welsh dresser that took pride of place in the kitchen. She set the table with accustomed ease. She'd been setting tables and serving lodgers almost from the time she could walk. She soon had everything they would need set out on one end of the long kitchen table.

"Sit down, Mam." She held one of the kitchen chairs away from the table. "Rest your feet for a minute." Her mother seldom had time to sit down.

"Tell me quick before the boys invade." Claudia almost groaned aloud at the relief of taking the weight off her feet.

"Mrs Huxley explained to me that I am not of the class of woman the Wrens will need." Vicky looked at her mother with dry eyes. "She suggested I lower my sights considerably."

"*The auld besom!*" Claudia gasped. Her daughter was as good if not better than all of them toffs put together.

"No, no, Mam." Vicky joined her mother at the table. "Mrs Huxley was kind. She wanted to save me disappointment, I'm sure."

"I never thought of Mrs Huxley as a snob." Claudia wanted to scream her rage to the ceiling. "She married beneath herself and look at her now – running a school out of her house. How dare she think she is better than us!"

"Mam," Vicky pushed her chair back and stood – the tea must be brewed by now, "me dad would say you're letting your redhead's temper run away with you."

"Redhead, me eye! I'll not let anyone talk down to my children."

Vicky poured a little milk into the two cups and then

poured a golden stream of steaming tea into each.

"Mam, Mrs Huxley said I let myself down every time I open my mouth. Besides all that, take a good look at me." Vicky stood with her arms out to her sides before turning slowly around. "Me skirt has that many little bobbles of gathered wool on it you would think it was made that way. Me jumpers falling apart." She sat at the table and put her hand over her mother's. "I don't mind – really I don't. There is many worse off than me but I can't apply to the Wrens looking like this."

She hated to be the cause of the despair she could plainly see on her mother's face.

"Don't," Vicky leaned towards her mother. "I know how hard it has been for you letting me stay in school so long and then going to secretarial school. I could have been out earning and you had every right to demand that, Mam, but you didn't. I don't feel hard done by – honest I don't."

"Your soul-sucking grandparents Nixon!" Claudia bit out between clenched teeth.

"Mam, what do you mean?" Vicky had never heard her mother say a word against her in-laws before.

"You're old enough to know what goes on around here, Vicky." Claudia pushed her cup away from her. The way she was feeling she wanted to throw the cup against the wall and if she started she wouldn't stop there. "I work me fingers to the bone seven days a week so I can send that pair the money they demanded before they would let your dad and me have this house. I wish to God your dad hadn't wanted to stay in his family home. We would have been better off seeking a place in service. That pair sit in luxury down there in Cornwall with their cronies, all the while crying poverty to your dad."

"Mam, I thought Dad's parents gave you this house!"

"Did they heck-as-like!" Claudia couldn't remain silent. She just couldn't. It was more than a human should have to bear. "They sold us this house at top market value. They didn't give us a family rate – oh no – the auld sods wanted their pint of blood. I have to pay them monthly and it takes nearly everything I make to keep them down there. I don't want them under me feet, I can tell you."

"But me dad is always saying how good his parents are to the two of you." Vicky had heard her father many a night singing the praise of his parents.

"Have you never noticed I leave the room when yer dad starts talking about his sainted parents?" Claudia sighed.

"I never thought about it." Vicky tried to remember all of the evenings the family had sat around the kitchen table and talked. "You always have so much to do."

"So I do." Claudia looked at her daughter, her heart breaking. She shouldn't lay her worries on Vicky's young shoulders but she just couldn't remain silent. "Oh, Vicky, if you had known your dad when I first met him! So tall, so handsome, always with a twinkle in his eyes. He was a dreamer but he never expected anything for nothing. He was going to work hard and the pair of us were going to conquer the world." She shook her head at the innocence of youth. "When he came home from the war with his lungs almost destroyed, it broke my heart. But he had come home. There was many that didn't. I couldn't moan and groan about me lot in life. It would have destroyed him."

The kitchen door flew open and even before it was fully open a voice called, "What's for dinner, Mam? We're starving!"

Two handsome boys appeared in the open doorway, a cheeky grin on each face. Nicolas at twelve years of age was the image of his father and his black hair and grey eyes were attracting the attention of the girls already. His brother Frank, a year younger, was so much like him people often mistook them for twins.

"Put your things in the sitting room." Vicky pressed her hand onto her mother's shoulder, stopping her from jumping to her feet. "I'll add water to the pot and you two can have a mug of tea and a lump of chuck to see you through to mealtime." A lump of chuck in the Nixon house was a thick slice of bread covered in dripping from the many roasts Claudia made for the lady lodgers.

"What's wrong with you two?" Frank stopped to look at his mother and sister. "You look like you lost a crown and found sixpence." He didn't wait for a reply but followed his brother into the family room off the kitchen. They were soon back in the kitchen longing for something to eat.

Vicky added water to the teapot. Her brothers didn't care what the tea tasted like just as long as it was hot and wet. She took down two mugs from their hooks and set them on the table, then pulled a tin loaf from the breadbox and cut two thick slices.

"What's up?" Nicolas dropped down onto a kitchen chair, looking from his mother to his sister. Frank joined him, saying nothing but looking from one woman to the other.

"Mam was about to tell me some home truths when you two exploded into the kitchen." Vicky fetched the thick jar her mother stored the dripping in from the cool room. She spread the dripping thickly onto the bread and with a flick of her wrist sprinkled salt over the top. She put each slice on a plate and put them on the table in front of her brothers.

"Eat them slowly so your stomach knows it has had something," she ordered, as her mother always did.

"What home truths?" Nicolas demanded, looking at his mother's bent head. She was staring into her lap. That wasn't a bit like his mother.

"Did you two know that Mam has to pay almost every penny she earns to our grandparents Nixon to pay for this house?" Vicky wasn't going to let this go. They needed to know what was going on. She'd heard her brothers moaning and groaning about the things they needed and wanted. It wasn't fair to her mother to make her the bad guy in this house.

"Vicky... no!" Claudia groaned.

"What's going on, our Vicky?" Frank watched Vicky pull their mam's cup closer to her and fill it with tea. She did the same with the boys' two mugs.

"Mam, me dad won't be in for ages. I'll help you with the lodgers' dinner. We need to know what is going on – Lord knows these two think they know everything." She jerked her chin towards her brothers.

"Tell us, Mam," Nicolas and Frank said almost at the same time.

"I never wanted you children to know." Claudia raised her head, her face paper-white, dark half-moons under her green eyes. That it should have come to this! "If any of you say something to upset your dad I'll never forgive you. So, think before you open your big mouth, Nicolas." She loved her children but she never had any doubts about their faults.

"Just tell us, Mam," Nicolas gulped his tea to wet his suddenly dry throat.

Claudia put her elbows on the table, shocking her three children. Elbows on the table – that was strictly forbidden. She dropped her head into her hands, her shoulders shaking.

Vicky put her arms around her mother's shoulders, offering what comfort she could. The two boys stared, unsure of what they should be doing. They had never seen their mother like this.

"Mam," Vicky rubbed her mother's back, "just tell us. We're big enough and bold enough to handle the truth. Whatever it is."

"It's all this talk of war." Claudia squeezed one of Vicky's hands and sat upright to stare across the table at her two sons. "It has been bringing back so many memories. Not just for me and your dad but for everyone who lived through the last lot."

"So that's what has you so upset?" Frank shoved the last of his bread into his mouth. He was still hungry but knew better than to ask for more.

"I met George just after the outbreak of war. He was already in uniform. So handsome, eighteen years old and a man of experience in my eyes. I was sixteen and starstruck. We fell in love while the young men of Britain were still thinking of the war as a great adventure." There was no need to tell them of the horrors that followed. George hadn't been in the fighting. The first two years of the war he had been a supplies officer. Then women had taken over those jobs and every able-bodied man had been sent to the front.

"I always thought it was so romantic that you married me dad before he left for the front." Vicky looked at her brothers with worried eyes. It was like pulling teeth, getting information out of their mother.

"I was eighteen, your dad twenty." They had to wait as both sets of parents had refused to give their permission for the marriage. When George was posted overseas they finally relented. "I lived in my parents' back bedroom in the East End of London while George served."

"Why?" Nicolas asked. "This house is huge and it wasn't a boarding house then, was it?"

"I had my family around me in the East End." Claudia had never felt welcome in this house. "Me sister and her children moved in while her husband was overseas – we needed each other to make it through each day."

"Your family were wiped out by the Spanish flu, weren't they?" Nicolas's voice was soft. He had never known his mother's family. Their untimely deaths were interesting but not emotional for him.

"Indeed." Claudia couldn't begin to share the horror of that time with these youngsters. Her husband returned a wreck of a man, struggling for every breath. Her sister's husband had been killed in the war. She had thought the worst had happened. Then the Spanish flu swept through the world, wiping out whole families. Her parents, her sister, the children – she had nursed them all – watched each one struggle for breath – then stood and watched them committed to the earth. George had been in a nursing home in the country. She had been unable to visit him for fear of contagion.

"And you survived all of that, Mam!" Frank looked at his mother with new eyes. He had always known, he supposed, that she had lost her family but it had been something of interest to him – not personal.

"There was many a one like me." Claudia pushed away from the table. "I have to get the dinner ready for the lady lodgers." She looked at her children. "And I suppose you lot will be wanting something to eat and all." She'd had enough emotional torment. She would tell her children about the house – she would – just not now.

Chapter 7

At the same time, in another part of London, Krista and the twins David and Edward were kicking a ball around the grass of the park that formed the inner section of the square the Caulfield and other homes surrounded. They were not alone in the park. The people of the square were enjoying the late-afternoon sunshine.

"*To me, to me!*" David yelled, running as fast as his little legs could manage.

Edward, sweating with his hair almost glued to his head, kicked the ball to Krista.

"*You were supposed to pass it to me!*" David clenched his fists and with fury in his green eyes started towards his twin.

"Gentlemen, is that any way to behave?"

"*Daddy!*"

Argument forgotten, two little whirlwinds ran towards the male whose commanding voice had broken up the argument before it could get started.

Krista spun around, the lightweight skirt of her navy-blue dress swirling. Captain Caulfield and Lia were standing arm in arm inside the entrance to the park.

The captain allowed the boys to tackle him off his feet and proceeded to roll around the grass, wrestling with his exuberant sons.

Lia walked over to join Krista, the two women enjoying the sight before them.

"A surprise visit – he arrived this morning after you had taken the boys to school," Lia said softly. "Some additional training and whatnot." She was of course thrilled to see her husband but in spite of his inability to give her details of the cause of his visit – she could guess – her thoughts and fears were hidden behind her smiling face. "You may go freshen up if you wish." Lia never took her eyes off her husband and sons. These moments were too few and too precious. "I will watch the boys." She sank onto a nearby bench.

"Thank you." Krista would have liked to stay in the small park and enjoy the sunshine but it felt intrusive. She hurried back towards the gate without calling goodbye to the boys. They were enjoying themselves and didn't need her.

***

"You caught me with my feet up," Peggy said when Krista stepped into the kitchen.

"Anything cool to drink? It is a beautiful day but I have been running after the boys and am sweating."

"Ladies don't sweat, Krista!" Peggy laughed. "They *glow*, don't you know that?"

"I am not a lady then because I am sweating." Krista stepped into the pantry, searching for something other than water to cool her thirst. "What is there to drink?"

"The iceman came yesterday. I've spent the morning breaking up those ruddy great blocks of ice and carrying refreshments up the stairs. My back is aching and my legs are talking to me." Peggy wasn't willing to move. She would have to jump up as soon as the family returned. In the meantime, she was going to rest her aching limbs. She had carried more trays up and down the stairs today then she normally did in a month of Sundays. Having a man in the house made more work for everyone, it seemed to her. Still, the captain and the missus deserved their private time and it was none of her business if they stayed in their room half the day. "There is a bowl of broken ice under the sacking in the back of the pantry. Bring out a bottle of lemonade when you're coming. We'll each have a glass of that while we have a minute to ourselves."

Krista returned to the kitchen to fetch two wide-mouth glasses. She filled these with ice from the bowl and with a tall bottle of lemonade under her arm returned to where Peggy sat at the table pulled to one side of the kitchen where the servants took their meals.

"Mrs Acers left a salad for the family to enjoy this evening." Peggy watched Krista pour the lemonade, her mouth watering.

"Is that what is under the pyramid of plates in the pantry?"

"It is. I have my instructions but Mrs Acers laid it all out before she left for the day." Peggy gulped at the lemonade Krista passed to her, the ice rattling against her teeth. It was quite a luxury to her to have ice for her drink. "Are you off for the rest of the day then?"

"I don't know." Krista sipped her drink, enjoying the fizzy bite of the bottled lemonade that was delivered to the doorstep with the milk bottles each morning. "I left the boys wrestling with their father on the grass." She shrugged. "I don't know what they plan for the rest of the day. I suppose I will just have to wait and see."

"If I was to guess," Peggy held out her glass for more lemonade, "I think you will be free for the rest of the day. The family don't get a lot of time to spend together – bless them."

"*Krista!*"

"*Krista!*"

"*Where are you, Krista?*"

"In the name of goodness!"

Peggy and Krista jumped from their seats, Krista running from the kitchen into the hallway. Surely the pair hadn't escaped the watchful eyes of their parents?

"Did you boys cross that road alone?" She stood, hands on her hips, glaring down at the happy pair.

"Daddy watched us," David said.

"Every step of the way," Edward added.

"We have to tell you something." That was David.

"Mummy said we could all have a drink of lemonade in the park." Edward was almost bouncing with excitement.

"Daddy said could you please carry the drinks over to us?" David looked at his twin in delight.

"Mummy wants you to join us," Edward said.

"Heavens above!" Krista was frantically wondering how she could carry tall glasses of iced drinks across the road without dropping them while keeping a careful watch on her two charges.

"Mummy says would you please bring our picnic blanket?" David stood, his head tilted as he tried to remember all of their instructions.

"And I am hungry." Edward took Krista's hand and swung it back and forth. "Could we please have something to eat?"

"Why don't you take that pair back across the road, Krista?" Peggy, standing in the open door of the kitchen, suggested. "We can sort ourselves out when you get back."

"Krista," Peggy pushed open the door into the kitchen, "you are wanted in the drawing room."

The two young women shared an uneasy glance. They had been running around frantically for what felt like days but was in actual fact hours. The twins were in bed, exhausted after an afternoon of high delight –

picnic in the park – football with their father – ice cream from a passing vendor. Then dining with their parents in style at the dining-room table. They had been overexcited and difficult to get to sleep but finally they were tucked away and Krista had come to the kitchen to share a well-earned pot of tea with Peggy.

"I thought they were going out?" Krista whispered as she stood away from the table.

"And so they are," Peggy said. "The pair are done up like the dog's dinner, ready for a night on the town."

"What do they want with me?"

"I'm sure I don't know but you better get in there." Peggy almost pushed Krista towards the kitchen door.

"I can't go in there, looking like this." Krista looked down at her bare legs. She hadn't changed her rumpled dress.

"Will you just get in there, for goodness' sake? The sooner you do, the sooner that pair will leave and I for one am ready for a bit of a sit-down. I'll put the kettle on and have the tea ready for you when you come back." She pushed against Krista's back. "Now, away with you."

Krista stood in the open door of the drawing room. "You sent for me?"

Lia, standing in front of the open windows, was almost a stranger in a full-length pearl-silk evening gown with diamonds glittering from her neck, ears and wrist. The captain in black tie was the perfect male companion to her stunning elegance. To Krista's eyes the pair looked like something from a magazine cover.

"Come in and close the door Krista, please." Charles Caulfield, silver ice-tongs in hand, turned from the cocktail cabinet where he was preparing drinks. His green eyes so like his twin sons glittered in his sun-kissed face. "I wish to speak with you. You may close the windows and pull the drapes."

"You look stunningly beautiful, Lia," Krista whispered as she passed her employer on her way across the room to close the long sash windows and pull the heavy drapes.

"She does indeed look beautiful, Krista, but then to my eyes my wife always does." The tinkle of ice dropping into glasses accompanied the captain's words.

"Should we turn on the lights, darling?" Lia took the sweating glass of gin and tonic from her husband's hands.

"Yes, of course," Charles used the back of his fingers to press a caress against his wife's face. "If you would, Krista? Then join us. Would you care for a gin and tonic?"

"Thank you but no, sir."

Krista moved around the room, switching on lamps while looking at the pair out of the corners of her eyes. Were they going to stand around the cocktail cabinet?

She stepped over to join them.

"Krista," Lia sipped her drink, "I have asked my husband to have a word with you. He does not know you as I do and is feeling rather uncomfortable. I have advised him to behave as if you were a midshipman."

"Darling!" Charles Caulfield wanted to pull at the

tall starched white collar around his neck. His wife was a delight but, really, it wasn't the done thing for him to speak to the help.

"Oh, for heaven's sake, Charles!" Lia almost slammed her glass onto the marble top of the cocktail cabinet. "My husband has been ordered to present himself for special training – in Norfolk, as it happens – his home county. The family are going to join him. We will be staying in the main house on my husband's family estate. The boys will love spending time with their grandparents. It will be a chance for us to be together for some weeks and I for one can't wait." She smiled at her husband, knowing she would be getting an earbashing for her candour.

"Am I to accompany you, Lia?" Krista wasn't sure she wanted to travel to Norfolk.

Charles was dashed uncomfortable. He had been ordered to have his family packed and moved to Norfolk. The London house – on the Admiralty's orders – was to be closed and the young woman staring at him with big bewildered blue eyes was to be made homeless. He had no idea why and hadn't asked. He was a captain in the King's Navy. He followed orders. He did not question them but it was the first time the Admiralty had interfered in his family's affairs. Did they believe he housed a spy?

"It would appear that someone in command wishes me to abandon you!" Lia was furious.

"Darling ..." What on earth was going on? Surely if the Admiralty had a concern about this young woman being a spy it would be better to keep her where they could be sure of her movements? Churchill was insistent that they should prepare for war. He had been First Lord of the Admiralty in the Great War and had the ears of a great many of the higher echelon of the navy. In the Great War Churchill had ordered seaplanes. Was that what his new orders were all about? He had never questioned orders in the past and would not now at what all those in the know believed was the rumblings of another war.

"Charles," Lia snapped, "Krista has no home of her own and no family. I will not throw her out to the mercy of whoever is working behind the scenes to get their grubby hands on her." She threw one arm in the cringing Krista's direction, her bracelet catching the light, throwing off flames of brilliance. "She speaks fluent German and French and while in our home her English has improved vastly. Do you not find the Admiralty's interest in our boys' nanny a little more than suspicious?"

The Grey Man! Krista almost said it aloud.

"Lia," Krista smiled at the woman who had become her friend over the last months, "do not upset yourself. Go out and have a good time. You look wonderful and it is not often Captain Caulfield can show you off."

"Oh, really –"

"We can talk about all of this some other time." Krista needed to think about the latest bump in her road. "Go out and enjoy the time you have together – please – do not worry about me."

"Sound advice, darling." Charles said.

"Oh, very well!" Lia could see that Charles wanted nothing to do with the problem of Krista. She would work around him. It wouldn't be the first time. "Where are my evening gloves and bag?" She looked around as if expecting the items to run towards her.

"I believe I saw them on the hall stand." Krista was glad to get away. "Let me get them for you."

After Krista left, Charles took the arm his wife held out and began to remove the diamond bracelets from her wrist. He would replace the bracelets when Lia wore her long satin evening gloves. No words were necessary, this was a familiar husbandly chore he much enjoyed.

"I cannot believe you just put me through that, Lia."

"There is more going on here than meets the eye, Charles."

"I am not a fool, darling." Charles green eyes glared into his wife's pale blue. "But it is not my place to question orders."

"Well, it is not my place to take orders."

"Here we are!" Krista stepped into the room, the soft leather evening clutch in one hand the long satin gloves in the other.

Chapter 8

Krista sat on the bed in her room, her back to the headboard, clasping her knees to her chest and desperately trying not to rock back and forth wailing like a mad person. She wished she could go to the large park just streets away and walk away her inner turmoil. She wanted to run screaming through the streets but she had to remain here to listen for the twins. That was what she was paid for after all.

What was she to do? She had been in this position once before. She had fled everything she knew in Metz. She had fled without a chance to plan, with only the clothes she wore and the coins from the mornings sales in the café of the Auberge du Ville in her pocket. She had travelled to England without papers, entering the country illegally. She was far better off now. She needed to count her blessings and not sit here like a gibbering idiot.

"*Come on, Krista*," she whispered aloud to herself. She rolled off the bed and stood examining the well-furnished room Lia had provided for her. "Time to try and plan your own future." She had been drifting along, feeling no need to step out of her safe little niche – now this!

"I have luggage and something to pack into it this time." She went on tippy-toes to remove the large suitcase from the bottom of the pile of luggage on top of the wardrobe. She checked the suitcase for dust before throwing it on top of the bed. She opened the case, staring unseeing for a moment into its depths.

"I have clothing ..."

She gave herself a mental shake. Standing still would achieve nothing. She opened the wardrobe doors, staring at the selection of quality clothing she had amassed in her time with the Caulfields. "I can pack my winter clothes now, with this warm weather hopefully they won't be needed." She left the wardrobe doors open and moved to the tallboy standing against the wall. Opening the bottom drawer, she began to remove woollen jumpers and placed them in the suitcase. She added her other heavy clothes.

"Shoes and boots ..."

She pushed her hands through her hair, staring down at the winter skirts, slacks and jumpers she had packed into the suitcase.

"I can't put shoes and boots on top of clean clothes.

I need to brush everything carefully and wrap them." She spun around. "Everything I need to do that is in the boot room." She pulled the door of her room open, standing for a moment in the corridor, listening. She opened the door to the twin's bedroom and stepped in for a moment, checking all was well. The boys were so adorable when they were asleep.

She ran back into her room to put on her slippers. Peggy would kill her for running over her polished floors in her bare feet. She ran down the stairs, along the hallway and into the kitchen. She stopped abruptly, the kitchen door swinging at her back. Everything suddenly hit her. The strength went from her knees. She was being forced out of her comfortable little world. She wouldn't see the twins again. No more tea in the kitchen with Mrs Acers and Peggy. Tears rolled silently down her cheeks. She almost stumbled over to the kitchen table she'd shared so many times with the others. She collapsed into a chair. It was over. What would she do? Where would she go?

"There is no time to be maudlin, Krista."

She wiped the tears from her face with her hands. She didn't know why she had this feeling of impending doom. She only knew that she would not allow the Grey Man – if it was he – to find her shaking in her shoes. She was so much better off now than she had been when she first fled oppression – if the Germans couldn't fell her, she'd be darned if the Grey Man succeeded.

"I have money in the Post Office," she stated aloud to the room.

Peggy knew nothing of this evening's revelations. She was visiting with the maid next door and would not be back for some time. She could speak aloud to herself as much as she liked. There was no one to hear her. She was glad she'd put her savings in the Post Office. The Grey Man might well have been able to freeze any funds she had in a bank – not that she would be allowed open a bank account – she was under twenty-one, the legal limit for handling your own accounts.

"I have a British passport if I should need it."

Her eyes roamed the room, committing its familiar features to her memory. She would miss this room and the friendship she had found here.

"Thanks to Lia's insistence, I have qualifications now." She bit back a sob. "I am a trained shorthand typist." She stuck out her tongue childishly. "So *there*, Mr. Grey Man!"

She needed to find somewhere to live. She would not allow herself to become homeless and at the mercy of anyone willing to provide a roof over her head.

She needed a home address if she were going to apply for a position as a secretary. She pushed herself slowly to her feet, feeling ancient.

"This won't get the baby a bonnet, as Mrs Acers would say."

"I haven't even looked at these." Krista took the large brown envelope Mrs Huxley had given her from the drawer of her dressing-table. She was shaking. So much had happened since she'd said goodbye to her school friends. She had forgotten all about the listing of situations vacant Mrs Huxley had given her. "I can't look at them now. I am exhausted." She looked to where she'd stored her one packed suitcase against the wall before beginning to restore order to the room. "I'll read it in the morning. When my mind is more at ease. Everything looks better in the morning."

The morning brought mayhem. The boys were almost impossible to get off to school. They wanted to remain with their father. Krista had to practically frogmarch the complaining twins out the door and on to their school. Would Lia tell Peggy and Mrs Acers that the house was to be closed up while Krista was out with the twins? She felt so guilty. What would Lia do? It was so unfair. She was being forced to close her home because of her. She had no doubts about that. Why was someone going to so much trouble to make her homeless and without income?

"We wanted to stay with Daddy!" David kicked at a stone in his path.

"*It is not fair!*" Edward said, his bottom lip trembling. "We wanted to wave goodbye to Daddy!"

"Come along, boys." What could she say or do? "You don't want to be late for school." The twins had only a few days left of their first year of school. Who would be walking them to school in September?

"We don't care," David insisted.

"Well, I do." Krista took each of them by the hand and hurried her steps. "I don't want the teacher to cane me."

"Silly!" Edward shouted with laughter. "The teacher would never do that."

"I am not so sure so come along, boys – shake a leg! We're going to be late." With a twin on each side of her, she hurried along the familiar streets, her heart lodged somewhere around her mouth. It would be so difficult to leave this pair of imps.

The school bell began to ring out and the threesome increased their speed to make it to the school before the gates were closed. They arrived panting in front of the main doors and with a hasty goodbye the twins disappeared into the wide opening, leaving Krista standing staring as the heavy doors were closed in her face. She turned away to stroll back to the Caulfield house.

"Krista, would you step in here a moment, please?" Lia appeared in the doorway of the drawing room. She had been listening for the key in the lock. Her eyes were red and there was a trace of tears on her white cheeks.

"Is everything all right, Lia?" Krista removed her jacket and hung it on the hallstand before following her employer into the drawing room.

"I am being silly." Lia wiped at her cheeks with her hands. "I have always known Charles went into dangerous situations when he left me." She took one of the soft chairs on either side of the fireplace, gesturing at the other with her hand. "All this talk of war suddenly hit me, I suppose." She waited for Krista to take the seat across the hearth from her before saying, "At least I waited to cry until Charles had left." She smiled sadly. "I am proud of myself for that at least."

Krista stared across the hearth at her employer, not knowing what to say or do.

"We need to speak of the situation we find ourselves in." Lia crossed her silk-clad legs. She put her elbow on the arm of the chair and jerked her chin towards the nearby coffee table. "Be a dear. Fetch me my cigarettes."

Krista was glad of something to do. She put an ashtray on the hearth in front of the empty fireplace. She lifted the large silver box of cigarettes from the coffee table and snapped open the top. She offered the open box to Lia. When she had taken a cigarette from the box Krista lit it from the silver lighter that was kept in one corner of the cigarette box.

"Thank you." Lia took a deep drag of the cigarette, her pale-blue eyes staring up at Krista. "Please sit down. You are making the place look untidy as Wilma Acers would say." She waited for Krista to sit. "As I have said, we need to speak. I am quietly furious at the situation being forced upon me ..."

"I am sorry –"

"It is not your fault." Lia held up the hand holding the cigarette in a stop sign. "I have not discussed the subject in depth with my husband." She closed her eyes while taking a puff of her cigarette. "Because quite frankly it would have degenerated into an argument of epic proportions. I could not allow that to happen." She blew smoke from her nostrils. "Someone is trying to force me to abandon you onto the streets of London. Someone very powerful if he can order the private life of one of his majesty's naval captains."

"I have thought the same," Krista said when Lia fell silent.

"I have been ordered to close my home." Lia leaned over the arm of her chair to smash her cigarette into the ashtray. "With no thought given to my staff. Mrs Acers and Peggy have been with me for years. Am I to turn them out too?" She planned to give Peggy the option of travelling to Norfolk with the family but the muckety-mucks didn't know or care about that!

Krista didn't know what to say.

"The boys of course will be delighted to spend time on their grandparents' estate. It will mean too that they get to see more of their father. Always a blessing. But it is I who will be left to handle the minutiae of closing up this house and moving my home to Norfolk. Whoever is pulling the strings here has not had the decency to discuss any of this with me. It is all jump and obey – but I am not a member of his majesty's service. Why should I bow down to whoever this is?"

"Lia, you took me in when I had nowhere to go. You supported me even when the police came to your home and carried me off. You have housed me, educated me, dressed me and cossetted me. I thank you for all of that from the bottom of my heart. However, it is obvious to both of us that my presence in your home is causing problems for you – that cannot be allowed."

"Can you not join one of the women's services that are being started up?" Lia thought this would be the ideal solution.

"That option is not open to me." Krista too had thought of enlisting in one of the many women's branches of the services. "You must have two British parents to qualify to serve. The people who organised my paperwork know my origins."

"That is unfortunate."

"I am frightened, Lia." Krista stared into the empty fireplace. "I did not tell you of my last meeting with the Grey Man."

"I thought his name was Brown."

"That is what he calls himself but everything about him is grey – his hair – his skin – his clothing. I always think of him as the Grey Man."

"I am sorry for interrupting you." Lia stood to fetch another cigarette. "I wasn't aware that you'd had more than one meeting with this Mr Brown." She puffed to light her cigarette and waited.

"It was while you were away over Christmas." Krista watched Lia walk across the room to join her. "He demanded my presence at Claridge's. He wished for me to ..." She had difficulty articulating just what the Grey Man had wanted her to do.

Lia waited, saying nothing as she puffed away.

"He wanted me to accompany a selection of high-powered foreign gentlemen to balls and galas over the holiday period. I was to listen to private conversations and report on everything I heard and observed. I am not sure if his intention was to have me seduce secrets from these gentlemen but that is certainly what it sounded like to me." Krista's face felt fiery red. She was mortified.

"Good heavens!" Lia choked on the mouthful of smoke she swallowed. When she had her breath back, she stared down at Krista. "He thought to turn you into a sort of modern day Mata Hari!"

"I refused."

"I should jolly well hope so. The nerve of the man!"

"I am not at all sure but I think the Grey Man is behind the sudden need to make me vulnerable to his plotting." The very thought of that had kept her awake last night.

"My dear Krista, that simply cannot be allowed!" Lia gasped.

"I do not know what to do. I fear that anything I try to do to gain employment and a place to live will be stopped by this man's finagling behind the scenes."

"Why on earth doesn't the man approach you face to face? There is no need for all this cloak-and-dagger carry-on."

"But that is very much what the Grey Man indulges in, I fear – cloak and dagger."

"Well, we shall soon put a stop to that," Lia stated firmly. "Time to call in the big guns – my sister-in-law. If anyone can get to the bottom of this it is dear Abigail. I daresay she knows just who this Grey Man is in real life." She laughed. "I would not put it past her to box the man's ears for him."

Chapter 9

"What is it, Pointer?" Clarence Brownlow-Hastings, his Burgundy velvet smoking jacket adding a touch of colour to his pale cheeks, puffed on a cigar, waiting for his butler to inform him as to the reason for this interruption.

"Lady Winchester has come to call, sir." Pointer stood ramrod straight in the open doorway of the elegant book-lined study. His disapproval of a married woman visiting a single male in the privacy of his own home almost visibly radiating off him. "I have placed her ladyship in the green withdrawing room. Are you at home to visitors?"

Clarence Brownlow-Hastings – the man Krista

called the Grey Man – wanted to beat his head off the cluttered surface of his desk. He was functioning on very little sleep. His eyes were burning in his head from reading badly written documents for hours on end. The last thing – the very last thing – he wanted to deal with was a visit from Abigail, Lady Winchester. He sighed, resigned to his fate – needs must.

"I do not suppose you can claim I am not at home." He glanced down at his at-home attire. She would have to take him as she found him.

"Of course he cannot." Abigail, beautifully groomed in an oyster-satin cocktail gown with matching jacket, her silk-clad legs gleaming, her hat a confection of lace and feathers, pushed the butler out of her path with a sniff and a glare. "Really, Clarence, I shall endeavour not to take up too much of your precious time. I do have other matters to attend to, other than hunting you down." She waved a hand dismissively at the butler. "You may leave."

Pointer glanced at his master.

"Yes, thank you, Pointer, you may leave." Clarence gave in to the inevitable.

"We do not wish to be disturbed." Abigail felt an imp of mischief sitting on her shoulder. She did so enjoy upsetting stiff-necked servants.

"Sir, m'lady." Pointer removed himself in a dignified fashion, closing the door softly at his back.

"You have upset my man, Abigail." Clarence leaned back in his leather desk chair. "You are looking well, my dear."

"A compliment sounds so much more gracious when not uttered through gritted teeth, my dear Clarry." Abigail had lost a great deal of weight in the last year. She was feeling so much better now that she had a purpose again. The sedate life of a lady of leisure was not to her taste.

"What do you want, Abigail?" Clarence sighed. "You have not travelled to Mayfair to hunt me down to exchange greetings. What brings you to my home?"

"Pour me a cognac and I will tell you." Abigail remained standing, looking around the study for a seat. There were two comfortable-looking chairs sitting in front of the desk. She refused to sit before his desk like a penitent. She leaned her hip against the desk, waiting.

"My butler could have served you." Clarence wanted to curse. The dratted woman would not leave until she got what she came for. He stood, turning to the crystal decanters sitting on top of a serving trolley close to his desk.

"It will not kill you to pour two brandies, Clarry."

"Oh, do sit down," he said over his shoulder. He poured brandy into two crystal balloon glasses.

Abigail turned the two chairs facing his desk around until they faced each other. She stood with her hand resting on the leather back of one, waiting for him to join her.

"You have always been a pest." Clarence turned, two glasses warming in his hands. He inhaled the aroma of Neapolitan brandy with pleasure. He walked around his desk, stifling a sigh at the amount of work awaiting his attention. He held out one glass, waiting for Abigail to take a seat. When she had seated herself and accepted the glass of brandy, he took the chair across from her.

"I have just come from the home of my sister-in-law, Cordelia Caulfield. She is most upset. Her husband – Captain Charles Caulfield of the Royal Naval Service – received orders from on high to close the family home in London and move his family to his parents' estate in Norfolk." Abigail sipped her brandy, her eyes examining the man before her for signs of deceit. Clarry had always been good at hiding his feelings. "Have these orders come from you?" She waited for him to answer.

He simply stared at her, his grey eyes revealing no emotion.

"Clarence, there is a time for secrets and there is a time for exchanging information. This is a time for sharing. Have you been interfering in my sister-in-law's private affairs?"

"I have not." His mind was frantically scurrying to add this information to his vast knowledge of ministry secrets. Who had made these demands and why wasn't he aware of the situation?

"You are sure, Clarry?" Abigail had been certain the orders had come from this man. Krista's Grey Man. If not him – who? "You have been showing an inordinate amount of interest in Constance's daughter."

"I want the chit under my command. I have made no secret of my interest," Clarence bit out. "She has talents that would serve me and my department well."

"Talents, Clarence?" Abigail leaned forward to glare. "Is that what you call it. It is my understanding you tried to get the girl to seduce men at your command. There is a name for women like that, Clarence, and there is an even more unpleasant name for the man who pushes them into such a position." She had been appalled when Lia told her what Clarence had suggested. "How could you even think such a thing of Constance's daughter? How, Clarry?" She gulped brandy to calm her nerves. She would achieve nothing if she physically attacked the man but she dearly wished she could.

"Do not be so dramatic!" Clarence snapped. "I merely suggested the girl could play escort to some very distinguished gentlemen. She would have enjoyed herself, I dare say."

"You used to be a better judge of character than that, Clarry." Abigail put her empty glass down, ignoring her hosts wince at the abuse of his highly polished desktop. That was what servants were for after all – cleaning up after those who employed them. "That girl, Krista, had young Peregrine Fotheringham-Carter panting at her heels. She could have reeled him in with the flick of her finger. She has countless young bloods snapping at her heels from what I understand." She flicked her foot against the leg of his pants.

"She travelled through Europe with Peregrine Fotheringham-Carter as man and wife." Clarence snatched the empty glass from his desktop. He carried both glasses over to the drinks trolley and barely restrained himself from smashing them. "She is not as innocent as you believe." He walked back to join the infuriating woman in front of his desk.

"Oh, Clarry, that girl is as innocent as the day is long. Any fool can see that just to look at her. Is this about Constance – still? Are you punishing the child for the sins of the mother?"

"Constance was to be my wife." Seeing that girl Krista had brought all of the anger he had felt when he was rejected back to the forefront of his mind. "She betrayed my trust. I agreed to postpone the nuptials as she insisted, until she had served her country. I did not expect her to continue that service after the war ended."

"How gracious of you!" Abigail would not allow him to pull the wool over *her* eyes. "Her travelling to Germany in an administrative capacity would not serve your future plans at all, would they?" She sighed deeply. This was all water under the bridge for heaven's sake. "You wanted to use her connections to advance your career in the Ministry of Defence. At least admit to it."

"That was beside the point."

"You were not honest with her, Clarry." Abigail could not believe that the conversation was returning to what she considered ancient history. *Men!* "Constance might well have married you, if only to give her child a name. If you had been truthful with her." She shrugged, staring at Clarence, sadness written over her face.

"I have no idea what you are talking about, Abigail." Clarence did not meet her too-knowing eyes.

"Was Constance to ignore all those pretty young

boys you surround yourself with, Clarry?"

"*I beg your pardon?*"

"Clarry, what you do in your private life is none of my business. But you should know you have not been as careful as you think you have been. Constance was never what one might call a fool. She deserved the truth."

"I have no notion of your meaning." Clarence resisted – barely – pulling at his cravat. His sexual preferences were illegal. The woman could send him to prison with just a word.

"Of course you have not." She leaned forward and touched his knee, almost laughing aloud as he reared back in his chair. "Just be more careful in future – please."

"Are we finished here, Abigail?" Clarence looked at his desk, avoiding her eyes. "I have much to do before I seek my bed."

"Are you speaking truthfully when you say you had nothing to do with the orders Captain Caulfield received concerning his family?" Abigail would not leave without his word of honour.

"I did not." He pulled the sleeve of his smoking jacket down, absentmindedly caressing the rich velvet as he spoke. "If you want to look elsewhere for your conspirator – look to Churchill – he has always been a friend to the Navy."

"Churchill!" Abigail gasped. She had given no thought to that man in the matter of Krista. "What on earth would Churchill want with Krista?"

"For heaven's sake, Abigail!" Clarence bit out. "You

were smarter than that in the day." He ignored her glare. "That girl speaks three languages fluently. She has intimate knowledge of the mood of the people in France and Germany. She is Germanic in appearance. She has no legitimate family – no protection from the powers that be. If she should suddenly disappear, who is there to question her absence? The papers she carries have been issued by an official of the Government. She is practically a gift-wrapped disposable tool!"

He ignored Abigail's gasps of shock at his coldblooded recitation of Krista's usefulness in the world of espionage.

"You will admit she is the perfect amalgam of her parents. She may well have her mother's face and figure but her white-blond hair and deep-blue eyes came from the man who fathered her, as anyone with eyes can see. She would be an impressive tool to wield in the coming conflict."

"Tool – dear Lord Clarry – what has happened to you?"

"Abigail," Clarence pinched the bridge of his nose, "every man, woman and child in Britain will be a tool in the coming conflict." He knew he could speak freely with her. The woman probably knew more about the secrets of the nation than he did. "The news being smuggled out of Germany is horrific. It would turn the stomach of any sane man. There will be no one safe if that man Hitler is not stopped." He shook his head sadly. "We are not equipped to stop him, Abigail – not yet."

"How did it come to this, Clarry?" Abigail stood. "I need more brandy." She took his glass from him.

"Allow –"

"Oh, do sit down, I am perfectly capable of pouring two shots of brandy," she said over her shoulder, not having to check to see Clarence had attempted to stand. "Answer my question."

"Hitler has been planning his attack since the end of the Great War. I am absolutely certain of that. The ink was most probably not dry on the Treaty of Versailles when Hitler and his cronies began planning their attack. The Great War never ended for some – the almost twenty years between then and now was merely a cessation in hostilities."

"Do you truly believe that, Clarry?" Abigail carried over the refilled balloon glasses. She gave him one before taking her seat.

"Yes, my dear, I do." Clarence closed his eyes and inhaled the aroma of the brandy. He opened his eyes suddenly, almost making Abigail jump. "I believe and I am not alone in my belief – that Hitler has been driving Germany towards revenge for what many see as the humiliation of the German people at the signing of the Treaty of Versailles. The man has been truly Machiavellian – his planning was inspired and insidious."

"You sound as if you admire him."

"No, my dear, I fear him. That is altogether a different matter." Clarence swirled the brandy in his glass, staring down into its rich depths. "The man has successfully brainwashed an entire nation. He has the German people hanging on his every word. Literally marching to the beat of his drum, high-stepping to the sound of his name. It sends shivers down my spine that one man – a very unattractive little man – has captured a nation with only the power of his own vitriolic words."

The two old friends sat in silence, lost in their own thoughts. They were powerless to change the future but both were determined to serve their country to the best of their abilities – in their own unique ways.

Chapter 10

Lia finally accepted the fact that she was not going to return to sleep – her brain was occupied with all she had to achieve in the coming days. She rolled out of her bed, shaking the twisted folds of her nightgown down to her feet. She almost stumbled over to the window. She pulled open the heavy curtains with a swish. The sky was barely light. She unlocked and pushed open the tall sash window of her room, inhaling the dew-laden air. The white net curtains would protect her modesty, hiding her from any passing traffic. Her bedroom overlooked the front of the house and over to the little park. She smiled at the sound of birds greeting the start of the day.

She turned from the window. It was too early to get dressed but she longed for a pot of tea. She pushed her arms into the dressing gown that matched her nightdress, tying the sash tightly at her waist. She slipped her feet into her leather slippers and almost crept from her room. The last thing she wanted to do was wake the twins. She wanted a pot of tea and a cigarette in peace before the house awoke around her. Peggy could have a lie-in on these bright warm mornings – there were no fireplaces to clear out.

In the kitchen Lia wanted to sing. It was so rarely she got the house to herself. She quickly put the kettle on to boil. She warmed the silver bachelor teapot and while the kettle boiled prepared a tray for herself. She stood back to examine her work: cup, saucer, ashtray, cigarettes, lighter, milk, sugar and slop bowl. She almost clapped her hands at the novelty of preparing her own tray. Such a small thing but with children and servants underfoot a rare treat. She made her small pot of tea and with a wide smile on her face carried the tray from the kitchen carefully. She did not want to clink dishes and wake anyone. She slowly mounted the stairs to her room, almost tripping over the skirt of her dressing gown.

In her room she put the tray on the bed and, feeling like a naughty child, pulled a small table over to the open window. She put the tray on the tabletop, poured the first cup of tea of the day and lit a cigarette before taking a seat on the wide windowsill.

With the brightening sky she watched the square

come to life. A newspaper boy on his three-wheeled bicycle, large wooden crate filled with the early morning editions of the nation's newspapers, pushed papers through letterboxes. Cleaning women, their hair covered by scarfs knotted to the front of their heads to mimic turbans, hurried along before disappearing into houses.

She heard the rattle of glass bottles before the appearance of the horse-drawn dairy float in the square. She watched the young man leap nimbly from behind the horse. He filled a tall-handled wire carrier basket with what must be the order for the first house on his route. He walked up each entryway swinging his basket, delivering milk, lemonade and whatever else was ordered to the door of each house. He removed the empty bottles from each doorway and whistling went on his way. She watched him make his way around the square, starting at the side furthest away from her house. It seemed her house would be almost the last of his deliveries. It delighted her to note that the horse didn't appear to need any direction but kept up with the young man as he went back and forth along the individual entryways to the houses.

Lia drank her tea and smoked her cigarettes, almost laughing aloud at the number of maids who appeared on the entryways, sweeping brush in hand. She couldn't blame them. He was a very attractive figure of a man from what she could see. She wished she had her opera glasses to hand. The man had a word and a smile for each maid who greeted him.

She had to stifle her laughter as her own maid Peggy

appeared under her window, sweeping the long entryway appearing not to notice the approaching milkman. Lia moved back from the window slightly, not wanting to be spotted but intrigued by the little drama being played out under her window.

"Good morning, Peggy!" the milkman called as he delivered four bottles of milk, cream and butter to the house next door to the Caulfield home. "How are you enjoying this beautiful morning?"

"Oh, Ernie!" Peggy turned to look at the smiling man raising his straw boater to her. She patted her hair, checking it remained in place under her white maid's hat. "I didn't see you there. It's all go this morning."

"Is it the usual this morning?"

"Mrs Acers left you a note." Peggy waved a hand in the direction of the empty milk and lemonade bottles sitting in front of the open door. One of the empty bottles had a white piece of paper sticking out of the neck.

"Did she now?" Ernie pushed his boater back on his head. "What's going on – not changing dairies, I hope." He walked down next door's entryway, his empty basket in hand and moved quickly to where Peggy stood.

"I told you – I don't know if I'm coming or going this morning," a blushing Peggy said as he stood close to her.

"What's going on then, young Peggy?" Ernie seemed to loom over the smaller figure of Peggy.

Lia didn't like his manner with her maid. She leaned against the wall to the side of the open window, ready to interfere if she didn't like what this young man said.

"You never made any mention of changes in the household when we went to the pictures."

To Lia's ears the man sounded almost accusing.

"I didn't know anything then, Ernie." Peggy smiled. "I'd have told you if I did. Haven't we been walking out together for weeks now?"

Ernie didn't answer, instead almost marching to the door and pulling the note from the milk bottle. "It says here I'm to make no deliveries to this house until further notice."

Lia couldn't see the milkman from her position but Peggy looked almost ready to cry as she looked at the young man.

"The family won't be here – the house is being closed up," Peggy offered with a shaky smile.

"When was this decided?" Ernie practically barked.

Lia didn't like this at all. What business was it of this man's what went on in her house?

"Ernie, what is wrong with you?" Peggy hadn't seen this side of her young man before. He was always such a gentleman. Always a smile and a cheery word. What was wrong with him this morning? "Did you get out the wrong side of the bed?"

"What's going on?" Ernie walked back to Peggy. He rubbed his hand gently down her arm.

"The family are going away. I have been asked to go with them." She looked at him under lowered lashes. "I am thinking about it."

"Where are they going?" Ernie snapped. "When was this decided?"

"Ernie ..."

"Is that foreign woman you told me about going with the family too?" Ernie wanted to throw his hat onto the milk float and run to the nearest public phone box.

"Ernie," Peggy objected, "you ask so many questions about my friend Krista that I am beginning to think you fancy her and not me."

"Answer my question!" Ernie took her elbow and shook her. "Is that foreigner leaving London? Did she get any more of them phone calls you told me about?"

"You make your deliveries, Ernie," Peggy pulled her elbow from his tight grip. She'd have bruises there later if she wasn't mistaken. She hurried into the house, avoiding his hand when he tried to grab at her. She almost slammed the door closed behind her. She was shaking. What was wrong with Ernie?

Lia watched the young man stand in the entryway with his jaw dropped. He didn't seem to know what to do.

"Everything alright, Ernie?" Mrs Acers said as she turned into the entryway.

Lia had been so involved in the drama that she hadn't noticed the approach of her housekeeper.

"Grand, Mrs Acers, grand." Ernie almost visibly shook himself. He grabbed the empty bottles from the doorway and hurried down the entryway, passing Mrs Acers.

Lia without a moment's hesitation ran to her wardrobe. She dropped her robe and nightgown on the floor. She pulled a pair of lightweight slacks from a hanger, and while hopping from one foot to the other she pulled the slacks up her legs and slid her feet into leather brogues. She riffled through a chest of drawers pulling a twin set and a silk headscarf out, with one eye out the window to keep the milkman in view as she dressed herself any old how. Ignoring the mess she'd made, she ran down the stairs

There was no sign of the milk float when she stepped outside her door. With a deep breath and walking swiftly she shook out the square of silk, folded it into a triangle and covered her hair. She was knotting the scarf under her chin as she stepped out of the square. It would not be difficult to follow a horse and cart surely.

She heard rather than saw the cart and ran in the direction of Regent's Park. The horse was standing at the kerb enjoying a meal from the nosebag someone had placed on its head.

"So, this is the last day you'll be wanting me horse and cart is it, young Ernie?"

Lia was almost caught. She had to do a quick step back before continuing to stroll towards the park. There was a tree close to the verge. She walked slowly towards it, straining to hear what 'young Ernie' had to say for himself. All she heard was a mumble.

"Strangest way to court a maid I've ever heard of," a deep voice said.

Lia hid behind the thick trunk of the tree. She couldn't risk putting her head around the tree to see the two men. The only sound to be heard was the horse chomping on whatever treat was in its nosebag.

"Still," from the sounds it seemed the older man was pulling himself onto the cart, "I've enjoyed the chance to grab a flask of tea in the park these last six months." He laughed then coughed huskily. "The missus thought it was romantic anyway." The reins being slapped against the horse's rump sounded. "Be seeing yeh, young Ernie. Be sure and invite us to the wedding."

If Ernie responded his words were swallowed by the horseshoes hitting the cobbles.

Lia waited before stepping out from behind the concealing trunk of the tree. The milk float was off in the distance but there was no sign of 'young Ernie'. She walked slowly back home, her mind in a whirl. Violet Andrews and Lia's sister-in-law had questioned how the movements of her household seemed to be known. They had never thought of the delivery men! Poor Peggy.

"A milkman!" Violet Andrews gasped. "Good heavens, whatever next?"

Violet, Abigail and Lia were sitting in Lia's drawing room, discussing what Lia had discovered that morning. Peggy had been obviously upset when Lia came downstairs that morning. Without asking the reason for the maid's red-rimmed eyes, Lia had given her the afternoon off and sent her to visit her family until the next day. She wanted Peggy out of the house while she met with Violet and Abigail to discuss the morning's revelation. Krista was picking the boys up from school and taking them for ice cream at a local

Lyon's tearoom. Mrs Acers had completed her day's work and returned to her own home. The ladies had the house to themselves.

"I had no idea of the number and variety of people that would have to be notified in order to completely close a townhouse down." Lia had served the ladies iced lemonade and she sipped from her own glass before saying, "I had Mrs Acers make me a list. It is quite extensive. There is the milkman, the coalman, the postman, the binmen, the boy who delivers the newspaper, the egg man, the butcher, the baker not to mention the window cleaner. The list goes on. Is it any wonder that the movements of a household can be easily checked!"

"I cannot imagine that Clarry would employ a man to play a lovelorn milkman," Abigail said.

"Clarry?" Lia raised her eyebrows and waited.

"Clarence Brownlow-Hastings to give the man his full name. The man Krista knows as Brown but thinks of as the Grey Man. He has been Clarry to me since we first met many years ago."

"Was he not engaged to Constance Stowe-Grenville at one time?" Lia vaguely remembered the gossip when the engagement had been broken. She'd been a romantic young girl at the time and inclined to sigh over the story of ruined romance.

"He was," Violet said.

"Never mind all of that." Abigail waved a hand. "We have more important matters to discuss. I asked Clarry – to his face – if he had ordered Lia from her home." She slapped the arm of her chair. "He categorically denied it. I believe him. This good-looking milkman does not sound like something Clarry would condone."

"It would appear there are multiple agencies interested in Krista." Violet's brows met over her eyes. She did not like the sound of this at all.

"If you could have heard Clarry make a list of the uses someone could put Krista to without anyone complaining! It sent shivers down my spine. He seemed to think the girl was a disposable commodity. To him she has no family to protect her. She is alone in the world. The fact that she speaks multiple languages and is attractive only seemed to add to what he termed her usefulness."

"We cannot allow Krista to be thrown to the wolves." Violet glared at the other two women. "I simply will not have it."

"What can we do to protect her?" Lia asked. "I am being ordered by my husband's superiors to lock up my home."

"Surely between us we can find her a safe place to lay her head," Abigail said.

"If only we had lied on her paperwork and claimed both of her parents were English!" Violet almost wailed.

"We would not have got away with it. Too many people know the story of her birth." Abigail had been tempted though.

"*Shh*, the children are back." Lia heard her boys chatter as they approached the house.

Chapter 11

"Krista, I did not think to see you back so soon." Lia stepped into the hallway, pulling the drawing-room door closed behind her. She had instructed Krista to take the boys for ice cream.

"Mama!" David struggled out of the shoulder straps of his schoolbag, allowing it to drop on the floor.

"Mama," Edward stood before his mother, smiling cheekily, "Krista said that we were sweating like little piglets."

The two boys thought that was hilarious and fell shrieking with laughter onto the cool tiles of the hallway.

"The boys' school uniform is simply too warm for this fine weather." Krista pulled the two boys to their feet. "I thought to give them a sponge down and change their clothing. We won't disturb you." She began to pick up the articles the boys had dropped.

"What is this I hear about sweating piglets?" The drawing-room door opened at Lia's back and Abigail, looking impossibly glamorous in one of the new-style coat dresses, stood smiling at the twins. "I have always enjoyed little piglets."

"*Aunty Abigail!*" the twins roared in delight almost knocking the woman off her feet as they threw themselves at her.

"Lady Winchester," Krista greeted the other woman, cringing when the titled lady was forced to hold onto the doorframe to remain standing.

"Krista, if you would like to get things ready this pair of hooligans can stay with us for a moment." Abigail smiled down at the delighted youngsters.

"Thank you, your ladyship." Krista said.

"Lia, you go with Krista," Abigail almost pushed Lia in the direction of the stairs. "Come with me, boys. I have iced lemonade." She pulled the two boys into the drawing room where Violet was already preparing two fresh glasses of lemonade.

"I am sorry, Lia," Krista said as the two women climbed the stairs. "I didn't know you had company but the boys really are much too hot in their heavy school uniforms."

The noise of the boys shouting over each other carried up the stairs. From the sound of it they were trying to tell all of their news to the two older women who were making much of them in the drawing room.

"Krista," Lia stood in the open doorway of the boys' room as Krista removed cotton shorts and short-sleeved shirts from the boys' dresser. "I have been wondering what positions Mrs Huxley recommended for you. Annora seemed to think you were much in demand yet you have made no mention of it."

"I haven't even opened that envelope yet." Krista was on her knees, reaching for the boys' bright-red summer sandals. "I had thought to look at it as soon as the boys are in bed this evening."

"Violet Andrews is downstairs with Abigail." Lia said. "I think you should take that envelope downstairs and perhaps discuss your options with them. I cannot leave London without knowing you are settled somewhere. I cannot simply desert you to your fate, Krista. So, for my sake if not your own please discuss your options with Violet and Abigail. They are wise old birds. I'll sponge the boys down and dress them if you will send them up."

"You certainly have options." Abigail, wearing a very attractive pair of gold-framed glasses, examined one of the pages she had removed from the large brown envelope.

Krista had removed the dirty glasses and melting ice from the drawing room. Violet and Abigail had decided to move to the dining room in order to spread out the papers. She was in the process of serving fresh drinks to the ladies.

"I am unsure," Krista placed cork coasters on top of the dining-room table before putting a tall glass of ice in place beside Violet and Abigail. "What should come first – a job of work – or somewhere to live?"

"It is a conundrum –" Violet began.

"Good heavens!" Abigail shook the paper she had in her hand. "Violet, quickly, have a look at this!" She held the page across the table. "Halfway down the page!"

"You will have to let the paper go!" Violet, her own glasses perched on the end of her nose, looked over the frames at her friend while trying to remove the page from her clenched fist. "You will tear it – let go!"

"I simply cannot believe it." Abigail held a hand to her heaving chest. "I had no idea. Did you?"

"Give me a moment." Violet wasn't a mind-reader she had no idea what had put her friend in such a tizzy. Her eyes searched down the page and became fixed on one name. "Reginald – a rear admiral – I had no idea."

The two friends leaned back in their chairs and simply looked at each other.

Krista didn't know whether to ask questions or wait a moment.

"Who do we know who would know?" Abigail tried to pull the page out of Violet's hand.

"Did you note the address?" Violet pulled the paper to one side. "Admiralty Building, Whitehall. What on earth would Reginald be doing there – and why does he need a trilingual secretary?"

"I am sure I don't know but we must know someone

who can give us more information – think, Violet – he is your brother after all." Abigail hated not to be in the know. How had she not heard of Reginald Andrews moving into naval intelligence? Which is where he must be – with that address.

"I believe …" Violet practically gulped air. "I believe the best way of dealing with this matter is by going directly to the source."

"Violet …"

Krista wondered what she was doing here. She could be helping Lia. The sounds of manic joy coming down the stairwell did not bode well. The twins were getting overexcited and would be difficult to handle.

"Abigail, they will not let us have her for the Wrens. I will not allow another service to profit from Krista's skills. The entire matter is becoming insupportable with shadow-agencies trying to force her compliance. We need information and if my brother has it – then by golly I am going to get it." Violet slapped the table to underline her determination. "You spoke to Clarry, Abigail – now it is my turn to gather information."

"Ladies, if you will excuse me." Krista had had enough. She didn't understand what these women were talking about and it was plain to her that they had no intention of informing her. "I will help Lia with the twins." She left the room without either woman objecting.

"Reginald," Violet tried not to be envious of the luxury that surrounded her. How on earth had her brother earned a flat in Admiralty House – were these flats not 'grace and favour' dwellings? Deeded to those who served the realm above and beyond the call of duty. She crossed the thick-piled carpet, hand out in greeting, very conscious of Reginald's batman at her back.

"Violet, it has been a long time." Reginald Andrews stood in front of the windows, his back ramrod straight. He examined his sister with pale-blue eyes that appeared enormous behind his eyeglasses. She was leading with her chin as usual. The woman could give lessons in stubborn. He stifled a sigh. Were they to indulge in one of the pitched battles his only sister had indulged in with their father?

"Father's funeral." Violet mentioned the last time she had seen her family.

"So it was." He gestured towards one of the deep chairs sitting close by the unlit fireplace. He waited until she had taken a seat before sitting himself. "I was surprised to hear from you." He looked at his waiting batman. "Can I offer you refreshments?"

"Tea would be lovely, thank you."

"I was thinking of something stronger."

"Thank you – no – tea will suffice."

"Tea for two, please, Dawson."

"Very good, sir." The door to the room closed softly.

"I am astonished to find you on dry land, Reginald." Violet examined her brother, making note of the many changes time had wrought. In the ten years since she had seen him his dark hair had silvered beautifully. The lines around his eyes and lips made him more attractive than ever. His upright figure looked trim and fit. The years had been kind to him. She looked around the opulent lounge. To her mind her brother didn't belong in this excessively furnished room. It did not suit the man she thought she knew. "I always thought that you would return to the family home when you quit the sea." She waved a hand around. "What are you doing here?"

"I am not here often." Reginald looked around the room. "You were fortunate to find me at home." He would not discuss the affairs of State with his sibling.

"Reginald, indulge me for a moment, please." Violet knew there was more going on here than met the eye. Her brother did not belong in these stuffy surroundings. He belonged on the deck of a ship. "What are you doing here?"

He was saved from answering by the return of his batman. The two remained silent while the man who had been at Reginald's side for years and knew most of his secrets poured tea and offered biscuits.

"That will be all, Dawson. Thank you." Reginald dismissed the man with a slight flick of the wrist that signalled all was well.

As his man closed the door, Reginald sat back in his chair, crossed his legs and sipped his tea. "You did not seek me out to chat about old times. Why don't you tell me what brings you to my door? Then we will see what is what."

"Very well." Violet unconsciously echoed her brother's movements. "Through happenstance today I found out you had been promoted to rear-admiral – congratulations by the way."

"Continue," he prompted when she stopped speaking.

"I was astonished as you will appreciate." Her brother had always sworn he would never accept a promotion that took him away from the sea. "I saw that you were seeking a trilingual secretary and couldn't for the life of me understand why. I have something of an interest in the matter so came directly to you to question what I consider a very startling occurrence."

"Indeed." Reginald put his empty cup and saucer on a nearby table before steepling his hands. "What on earth is your interest in my affairs?"

"I …"

"Before you get your tongue in a knot, Violet, just spit it out."

"How on earth do you handle the politics of your position, Reginald? You always were impatient." Violet laughed softly.

"Get on with it, woman."

"I know of a young woman who is an extremely talented trilingual shorthand typist," Violet offered.

"Do you indeed?" Reginald stared. "Tell me about her."

"Tell me first why you have need of someone like her?"

"I cannot." He held up his hand when she opened her mouth to object. "I cannot, Violet." He took off his cursed glasses and pinched the bridge of his nose. "I have been made aware of your work to reinstate your beloved Wrens. You know that not everything can be explained. I'm sorry. My need of young women with language skills is one of those things. In fact, many have been watching your enlistment lists with interest. The need for foreign languages is vital at this moment in time. You cannot be unaware of this matter, surely?"

"Reginald, the young woman I am concerned with – I consider her my ward – she is fluent in English, German and French and has some knowledge of Italian and Spanish. She has a driver's licence and has been trained in driving heavy vehicles. I cannot have her as one of my Wrens much as I would love to – her parents are not both British."

"You are not speaking of that dashed Lestrange chit, are you?" He leaned forward to almost glare at his sister. "The one young Winters sent into Europe to rescue his sister. Not that young woman. In the name of goodness, woman, everyone and his mother has been trying to lay hands on her." He turned his head to the door. "*Dawson!*" he suddenly shouted.

"Sir!" The batman almost fell into the room. He must have been standing outside with his ear pressed to the door.

"*Order my car!*" Reginald shouted as he stood.

Dawson stepped out.

"Just a moment." Violet jumped up too. She put her hand on her brother's chest, stopping him in his tracks. He pulled backwards, unaccustomed to anyone laying their hands on him. "We need to talk."

There was tension in the room for a moment as it

seemed the rear-admiral would ignore everything and storm ahead.

"I want that woman working for me. I have been fighting to get her under my command ever since I heard of her exploits in Germany. Brownlow-Hastings, not to mention Winters, has been blocking my every move and now you tell me you know her. She is your ward, you say – why, we are practically family!" His smile was tinged with such satisfaction Violet felt a shiver down her spine.

"Are you responsible for ordering Captain Caulfield to remove his family from London?" Violet demanded. "Are you the man trying to make Krista homeless? And that dreadful milkman romancing the household maid? Shame on you, Reginald! That is an abuse of power."

"A milkman? Woman, what are you talking about?" Reginald snapped. "Sit back down for heaven's sake and tell me everything. I want to know everything you know about this Lestrange chit – *everything*, Violet – leave nothing out."

Violet was shaken. She had not expected anything like this when she had called on her brother.

"For heaven's sake, Violet!" Reginald's tone was disgusted. "I want to use the woman's skills, that is all. Now, tell me everything."

"Pour me more tea then." Violet gave in. Krista would be safe with her brother. She would see to that. "This will take some time. I have known Krista since she was a small child growing up in Metz, France …"

Chapter 12

"Peggy, you don't need to take your maid's uniform with you." Krista pulled the items out of the suitcase resting on the bed in Peggy's room off the kitchen. "You are going to take care of the boys. You will need slacks and wellington boots."

"I don't know if I'm coming or going." Peggy dropped down onto the bed, a picture of misery. "I've never been on a train. I've never been to the seaside. What am I going to do on a country estate?"

"Come along, Peggy. Buck up." Krista pulled Peggy to her feet. They didn't have time for dramatics. "You have been with the twins since their birth. You know what they are capable of. Lia needs an extra pair of hands. She can handle the travel details. You can keep hold of the inquisitive twosome. You know they will have their little noses into everything."

"I don't know why she couldn't take them in the estate car as she has in the past." Peggy allowed Krista to hurry her along.

"The boys are too rambunctious to sit quietly in a car for hours on end. There is more room to run around on a train." Krista remembered Lia swearing not to travel alone with the boys in a car again if she could prevent it. "Come along, it will be an adventure."

"I don't know how you are brave enough to stay in this big house all on your own." Peggy allowed Krista to continue packing her battered cardboard suitcase. "I would be frightened of my life."

"It won't be for very long." Krista checked off the list of items she was convinced Peggy would need for her long stay in the country.

"A very strange sort of job you have taken if you ask me," Peggy muttered as she stuffed last-minute items down the side of her already bulging case.

"We shall see." Krista knew Peggy wanted more details of the position she had accepted with Rear Admiral Andrews. How could she tell her something she didn't know herself? She was waiting for a letter from the Admiralty with further details of her position. She was receiving a salary commensurate with what she would have received as an under-secretary in an office. That was important. She could not live on fresh air! "Peggy, I want to get some sleep tonight. The boys will be up bright and early, full of demands for things I have forgotten to pack for them, I don't doubt."

"I will never shut my eyes tonight," Peggy yawned widely. "I don't know how you can be so calm. The world is all topsy-turvy."

"Jump up on the case." Krista yawned along with her friend – it was contagious. "We will need your weight to get the locks closed. Thank goodness for the leather straps. If this thing bursts your belongings will not fly all over the place."

"Oh, don't say that!" Peggy shuddered.

Late the following morning Krista stood in the open doorway of the Caulfield house waving goodbye to Lia, the boys and Peggy. She was exhausted. The early hours of the morning had been frantic. The greater part of the family and Peggy's luggage was sitting in the hallway waiting for a postal delivery van that would take the items all the way to Norwich. This morning it was only a matter of arranging travelling cases and getting the boys fed, washed and dressed for the journey. Peggy had been worse than useless, her normal calm deserting her completely. It had been left to Krista to run around like a demented ferret getting everyone organised and moved along. If she hadn't to wait here for the delivery men she would have returned to her bed to recover from the sheer madness of the morning.

She waved until the taxi taking the travellers to the train station disappeared from view. With a heartfelt sigh she closed the door of the house and stood for a moment, examining the label-strewn luggage that formed a little mountain in the hallway. She made her way slowly to the kitchen and ignored the wreckage that awaited her. She would make a pot of coffee for herself before getting stuck into tidying up the mess. She put two large pots of water on to heat before taking a seat at the kitchen table – after clearing a place for herself. The boys had been overexcited this morning and a great deal of their breakfast was strewn over the tabletop.

The public rooms of the house were covered in dust sheets. Krista had to strip the beds and send laundry out. Then she would sweep the rooms out before covering everything in dust sheets, leaving only her bedroom and the kitchen uncovered.

So much had happened in so little time. Krista, at Violet Andrews' recommendation, had accepted a position as assistant to the rear admiral – her brother – and was awaiting final instruction. The position as far as she could understand was that of a roving secretary. The rear admiral had not been able to give exact details of the work involved but before she could take up her position she had to take six weeks training in Portsmouth. Krista had agreed, thinking it sounded a great deal more interesting than sitting in a stuffy office, pencil at the ready.

Coffee break over, Krista put a large wraparound apron of Mrs Acers over her summer dress and began the clean-up.

The doorbell rang when Krista was sweeping the kitchen floor – order had been restored to the room and she was feeling quite pleased with herself. She left the wraparound apron in place. She had a great deal more to do. She hurried to open the door.

It was the Post Office truck.

"Got luggage to pick up." The burly man consulted his clipboard.

"Yes, indeed." Krista opened the door wide, allowing the man to see the luggage stack.

"That little lot cost someone a fortune." He whistled between his teeth before turning his head in the direction of the large truck standing in front of the house. "*Gofer, come give us a hand! Bring the dolly!*" He turned back to Krista, not waiting to see if his shouted orders were being obeyed.

"I need to check this lot off, missus." He waited for her to allow him entry.

"Please come in." Krista stepped out of the way.

A young man pushing a metal trolley appeared, hurrying up the entryway.

Krista stood back and let the men get on with their job.

Krista hurried along Waterloo rail station, searching for the platform number she had been given in the letter from the Admiralty. She was dressed in a lightweight cotton navy-blue dress. A straw boater with a navy ribbon-band sat on top of her head and she had T-strap navy-blue shoes on her feet. She attracted attention as she strode across the apron of the station, silk-stocking-covered legs flashing. She had her bag across her body for safety and the letter – which she had memorised – was safely inside with the papers she had been instructed to bring with her. She waved off a porter. The case she was carrying wasn't very heavy. She'd been given detailed instructions as to what she was to bring with her in the way of clothing. She had thought that strange but obeyed to the last detail.

She saw a heavy-set woman wearing the strangest outfit she had even seen. The material the navy suit was made from was far too heavy for the fine weather London was enjoying. The long skirt and heavy double-breasted long belted jacket and tricorner hat squashed on her head made her stand out from the crowd of brightly gowned women standing at her back. The woman was stuffed into the suit like a sausage and was visibly sweating. She was standing, a clipboard in hand, legs braced apart, under the sign giving the number of the track and the destination of the train standing puffing on the rail. Portsmouth, that was the train Krista needed.

"*Right, ladies!*" the woman shouted in a voice like a foghorn as Krista approached the gate. "*It would appear we have our straggler!*"

At her words the women behind her almost exploded into action. Porters were shouted for, arms in brightly covered materials were waved in the air. Excited voices mingled into a sound like hens cackling and individual words were hard to make out.

"You are Lestrange?" the woman barked at Krista.

"I am Krista Lestrange, yes." Krista tried not to stare at the woman's hairy chin.

"Foreign." The woman sniffed unpleasantly. "One of Reggie's lot."

Hildegard Henderson wondered what she had let herself in for. These women had no discipline. They had been given strict instruction on what to bring with them but they were loaded down like debutantes on their way to a foreign holiday instead of mature women chosen to lead. This one at least had only one case with her. She supposed that was something. She turned to the women at her back.

"*Right, you lot, on the train!*"

"*I can't manage!*"

"*I need assistance!*"

"*Where are the porters?*"

The babble of voices continued to voice complaints. Krista stepped around them to walk along the waiting train. She had been given the carriage number in the letter she received. When she found the correct carriage number, she stepped up into the train. She put her case in the overhead space and removed her bag strap from around her head before taking a window seat. She was alone in the carriage for the moment.

"What a scrum!" A brown-haired woman struggled into the carriage from the corridor.

Krista jumped up to offer assistance.

"Andorra Prendergast," the brown-haired, brown-eyed woman offered with a slight smile as she stepped away from her heavy case. "Could you be a love and put that on that shelf-thing?" She waved a pale beringed hand towards the overhead storage. "That is frightfully kind of you. A darling porter is arranging my luggage in the luggage carriage. Much to the disgust of our esteemed leader. Honestly, have you ever seen such a fright?" She dropped down into a seat as if exhausted.

Krista stood looking down at the woman in amazement. Did she really think Krista would be able to lift her heavy suitcase over her head – alone! Start as you mean to go on, she thought, and returned to her own seat across the central aisle of the carriage.

"What are you doing?" Andorra Prendergast stared at Krista while removing cigarettes and lighter from her travel case which she had dropped on the seat beside her. "That case needs to be moved."

"It's your case. You move it." Krista wasn't anyone's servant.

"*What is that article doing blocking the aisle?*" Hildegarde Henderson stood in the open carriage doorway staring at the two who had dared to enter the carriage without her permission. "*Move it at once!*"

"I have told her it needs to be moved." Andorra puffed a smoke-ring into the air. "All of this rushing around – it is too terribly fatiguing."

"Lestrange ..." Hildegarde had known taking a foreigner on would be trouble.

"My case is in the overhead storage rack," Krista said before she could be blamed for something that was not her business.

"Prendergast!" Hildegarde barked. "I saw you give the porter a mountain of luggage." She paused to glare down at the woman. "You were given strict instruction as to what to bring with you." She kicked the case with her sturdy laced-up shoes. *"Move this thing or I will have it thrown off the train."*

"Don't be ridiculous!" Andorra sighed mightily. "That case contains my jewels and personal items. I would be lost without it!"

"Move it," Hildegard glared.

"Oh, very well but I do think you are being frightfully unfair." She threw her cigarette out the window, uncaring where it might land or who it might hit, and stood. "Well," she stared at Krista in disgust, "you offered to help."

"Help, yes," Krista remained seated. "Do it for you – no."

"Oh, for God's sake! Get that thing out of the aisle."

Hildegard wanted to pull her own hair out. This was a disaster and the train hadn't even left the station yet. She watched the two women struggle to get the suitcase into the overhead storage before turning and waving the rest of the group onto the train. They were still standing in the aisles, trying to get organised, when the train pulled away from the station, sending a screaming crowd into hysterics.

Krista could only stare in disbelief – what with falling bodies and luggage it was ridiculous. What on earth had she signed up for?

TO BE CONTINUED

Made in the USA
Middletown, DE
30 October 2024